Say Goodbye . . . for Good?

"Ooh, Tia. You might be getting a rich stepfather. Wouldn't that be cool?" Chantal said excitedly.

Tia shook her head. "It would be terrible," she said. "You haven't seen him. He's like a cartoon cowboy. He tips his hat and says, 'Yes, ma'am.' He's totally wrong for my mother. I just hope she's smart enough to see it."

"If she marries him, will you guys have to go live on the ranch in Texas?" Denise asked.

"Can you see Lisa living on a ranch?" Tamera giggled.

"It's not funny, Tamera," Tia snapped. "Don't you see? If my mother marries this guy, then I'll have to move away from here—away from my friends and my school and away from you!"

Books by Janet Quin-Harkin

SISTER, SISTER
Cool in School
You Read My Mind
One Crazy Christmas
Homegirl on the Range

TGIF!
#1 Sleepover Madness
#2 Friday Night Fright
#3 Four's a Crowd
#4 Forever Friday
#5 Toe-Shoe Trouble
#6 Secret Valentine

Available from MINSTREL Books

HOMEGIRL ON THE RANGE

JANET QUIN-HARKIN

Published by POCKET BOOKS
New York London Toronto Sydney Tokyo Singapore

A MINSTREL PAPERBACK *Original*

A Minstrel Book published by
POCKET BOOKS, a division of Simon & Schuster Inc.
1230 Avenue of the Americas, New York, NY 10020

ISBN: 0-671-00284-8

First Minstrel Books printing February 1997

10 9 8 7 6 5 4 3 2 1

Printed in the U.S.A.

Chapter 1

"I don't believe it," Tamera Campbell said as she sprawled back on the sofa. "It's Saturday afternoon, and I've got nothing to do."

Her twin sister, Tia, looked up from the dining table, where she was working. "How about a little thing called homework?" she asked. "It really is less stressful when you don't have to do it on the bus going to school on Monday morning."

"For your information, Miss Know It All," Tamera said smugly, "I have finished my homework." She looked around quickly. "I hope nobody heard me say that. If you tell anyone, you're dead."

Tia laughed. "Tamera, why should you be ashamed of having done your homework?"

"Because kids at school might think I'm turning into a brainy geek like you—and because my dad might start mouthing off again about what a good influence you've been on me."

"But I have been a good influence," Tia said. "Look how much better your grades are these days."

"Just my natural genius finally beginning to blossom," Tamera said. "I look on myself as a late bloomer."

Tia looked down at the book she was studying and tried not to giggle. "My sister, the chrysanthemum," she muttered.

"You should be proud of me," Tamera said. "It must be the first time ever that I have my homework done before you."

"I'm impressed," Tia said. "I don't know when you did it either. You were out at a movie last night, and you slept late this morning . . . and there was that whole long history assignment filling in dates and places. It's been taking me hours, and I'm still not done yet."

"I guess I'm just a speedier worker than you," Tamera said, pretending to examine her fingernails. "And I happen to know the right people."

"What right people?"

"Dahlia Burton. She sat with us at lunch yesterday while you were at your science club meeting. She's a junior, and she had the same assignment last year. She gave me hers with all the dates filled in."

"Tamera, that's cheating!"

"No, it's not, it's using my head," Tamera said, "and it's also using my time wisely."

"I don't think I want to talk to you anymore," Tia

said, sweeping her books together and getting up from the table.

"You don't want to talk to me because I got the answers to a long boring assignment that saved me hours?" Tamera asked.

"No, because you didn't tell me about it and give me the answers, too," Tia said. "Do you know how long it's taken me to look up all that stuff—you brat!"

She threw the nearest pillow into Tamera's face. Tamera started laughing, and Tia joined in. She went over to sit on the arm of the sofa. "So why don't you go out if you're all done with your homework?"

"Nothing to do. Nowhere to go," Tamera said. She sighed again.

"You mean you finally realized that the mall is a shallow and boring place to hang out?"

"No, but it's no fun alone," Tamera said. "I've already called everyone I know, and they're all busy. Besides, I have no money, and what's the point of going to the mall if I can't buy anything."

"Tell me about it," Tia said. "I'm flat broke, too. Just for once I'd love to be rich."

"Me, too," Tamera said. "I'd get a car the moment I pass the driving test, and a bigger stereo, and I'd buy every cute dress I saw in store windows."

"I don't even want that much," Tia said thoughtfully. "I'd just like to have enough money so that I didn't have to choose between going to a movie or going out for pizza or buying a new tank top. I can't wait to be sixteen and get a real job after school, if my mom will let me."

"Why wouldn't she let you?" Tamera asked.

"You know what high hopes she's got for me. She's already bought the Harvard sweatshirt—"

"And the Yale sweatshirt and about a dozen others. I remember," Tamera said with a grin.

"So she wouldn't let me do anything that took time away from my studies," Tia said. "She wants that Ivy League school as much as I do, more in fact."

"My dad wants me to go to a good college, too," Tamera said, "but I think he can just keep on dreaming. I'll be lucky if I make it to the local JC."

"You'll do fine, Tamera," Tia said. "If only you'd stop trying to find ways to get out of doing your work."

Tamera looked horrified. "But I wouldn't have any time to myself if I really did all my homework!"

"You've got time now and nothing to do with it," Tia said with a smile. "Why don't you go to a movie?"

"I saw the only good one last night," Tamera said. "Everything else playing right now is boring—you know, old-fashioned people talking to each other on the edge of a lake for two hours. Not my kind of movie at all." She looked up hopefully at Tia. "If you'd only stop doing that stupid homework, you could come out with me."

"I have to get an essay finished for English," Tia

said, "but I'll come out with you if you can think of something interesting to do."

"Did I hear anyone saying they wanted something exciting to do?" A voice echoed down the stairs. Lisa Landry, Tia's mother, came down the stairs with a big smile on her face. "I have a suggestion you're going to love!"

Tia and Tamera stared at her with their mouths open. Lisa was dressed head to toe in Western gear. She was wearing riding pants and boots, a checked shirt with a fringed vest over it, a bandanna around her throat, and a big Western hat. In her hand she carried a riding crop.

"The rodeo's in town, and you're about to try calf roping?" Tia asked, giving Tamera a despairing look.

"You're trying out for a production of *Annie, Get Your Gun?*" Tamera suggested, starting to laugh.

"No!" Lisa said angrily. "I am about to take my horseback-riding lesson, and if you girls are free, why don't you come along, too?"

"Mom, you tried horseback riding last fall," Tia said. "It was a total disaster. You got on backward, remember, and the horse started trotting away with you facing its tail and yelling 'How do you make this thing stop?' "

"Just a little mistake. I bet it happens to most people first time out," Lisa said.

"It didn't happen to anyone else in the class," Tamera commented.

"It was so embarrassing, Mom. All those people

laughing at you. I don't know how you can possibly want to try again."

"Because Lisa Landry never gives up," Lisa said. "I wasn't born a quitter. I've been thinking about horseback riding all winter and I made up my mind—as soon as spring came, I was going to learn to ride that horse. Well, spring is here and I'm ready. Pretty soon I'll be jumping over gates and galloping around."

"Yeah, and maybe one day you'll be able to do it on horseback," Tia said, nudging Tamera.

"You're my daughter, you're supposed to be out there, rooting for me," Lisa said indignantly.

"I am your daughter, and I care about you," Tia said. "I'll be out there, ready to catch you when you fall off again. But I don't see why you want to do this, Mom." She went over to her mother and put her hand on her mother's shoulder. "Why would somebody in the middle of Detroit want to learn to ride a horse? It's not as if it's ever going to come in useful in your life."

"It might," Lisa said.

"How?" Tia demanded.

"Maybe one day when I'm at the top of my fashion career, I'll be showing my collection in England and Prince Charles will invite me to take part in the local hunt," Lisa said.

"Yeah, that's a real possibility," Tamera said to Tia. "Right up there with being stung to death by killer bees."

"Okay, if you really want to know," Lisa said, sink-ing down to sit on the bottom step of the stairs, "it's all because of Carrie Harrington."

"Who is Carrie Harrington?"

"This prissy kid who went to grade school with me and took horseback-riding lessons. She didn't invite me to her birthday party, and you know what she said? She said there's no point in inviting you, Lisa Landry, because I'm having pony rides and you'd only make a fool of yourself. Everyone else has taken horseback-riding lessons except you."

"That is so mean," Tia said.

"She sounds like a total snob," Tamera agreed, "but why should it worry you now? It was all over years and years ago."

"Not all that many years," Lisa said quickly. "Anyway, it still hurts me when I think about it. I know it's crazy, but I have this fantasy of learning to ride really well and then going back home and galloping past Carrie Harrington."

"Mom, that's so stupid," Tia said. "You haven't been near that place for years. You don't even know if Carrie Harrington lives there anymore."

"I know," Lisa said, "but it's something I have to do. And a woman's got to do what a woman's got to do."

Tamera turned to Tia. "Why do I think that I've just stepped into the middle of an old Western movie and any moment now Lisa is going to saddle up and ride into the sunset?"

"Not facing the wrong way this time, we hope," Tia chimed in.

"Fine, go ahead. Make fun of me," Lisa said. "You girls go do your thing, and I'll go to my riding lesson by myself."

She stood up and headed for the front door. Tia looked at her sister. "We'll come with you if you like," Tia said.

"Yeah, horseback riding might be a kind of fun thing to do," Tamera agreed. "And it's a useful skill to know, just in case we meet any snobby girls who won't invite us to their birthday parties."

Lisa threw an arm around each of them. "We'll have a great time," she said. "And after the lesson we'll stop off at the ice-cream parlor and get a giant sundae."

"Now you're talking," Tamera said. "We'd do anything for a giant sundae."

"I just hope I can eat mine," Tia said. "Last time we all went horseback riding, my insides were still going up and down an hour later."

"I just wish they'd put steering wheels on horses," Lisa said, "but I guess we'll get the hang of it soon enough. If all those old movie stars learned to do it, then I'm sure we can, too."

The girls ran upstairs to change their clothes. When they came down again, they found Lisa waiting for them, sitting in her car.

"I just hope your car makes it as far as the riding stables today," Tamera said, as she climbed into the backseat. Lisa had finally bought herself an old Cadillac, but the girls secretly admitted that the salesman had sold Lisa a lemon. It smoked, it growled, and parts of it dropped off every time they drove in it.

"There's nothing wrong with this car," Lisa said proudly. "This car is a classic."

"So were Roman chariots," Tia muttered under her breath.

The whole car shook until finally the engine roared to life.

"We're off," Lisa yelled excitedly. "Any second now, we'll be riding into the sunset."

"Around here, you'd better watch that we're not riding into a brick wall or a freeway," Tia warned.

"I don't know how I managed to have a daughter who completely lacks my spirit of adventure," Lisa complained. "You're going to love horseback riding. Don't tell me you didn't like it last time you tried it. You seemed happy enough afterward."

"That was because it felt so good when we stopped," Tia said. Then she saw her mother's expectant face. "But I guess it will be more fun this time," she added hurriedly.

Chapter 2

"See—that was fun, wasn't it?" Lisa said as they handed their horses back to the stablehands and headed out of the stable yard. "And you girls did really well for your second time on horseback. And I wasn't too bad, was I? After that little incident, I mean."

"You did great, Lisa," Tamera said. "Imagine taking a jump on your second lesson. The riding instructor was so surprised!"

"I didn't intend to take a jump," Lisa said. "The horse behind me bit my horse's rear end, and suddenly we were heading for that jump at full speed."

"You managed to hang on, Mom," Tia said.

"You bet I did," Lisa agreed. "I was hanging on to that saddle horn for dear life. I expected to come flying off at any second."

"Actually, you looked pretty good," Tamera said.

"I did?" Lisa looked at her hopefully. "You mean sort of like National Velvet?"

"More like National Polyester, but pretty impressive," Tia said with a grin to Tamera.

"Maybe I do have a gift for this riding thing," Lisa said. "Maybe way back in my ancestry there was a Landry woman who galloped over the plains of Africa . . ."

"I don't think they had horses in Africa, Mom," Tia said, trying not to smile.

"Okay, so maybe there was a Landry woman who was in the Pony Express," Lisa said. "I just get that feeling in my bones that horses and I belong together. 'Oh, give me a home where the buffalo roam . . .' "

Tia shot an embarrassed look at Tamera. "Mom, please don't sing in the street," she said. "And don't you dare say 'howdee' and 'heehaw' when we go into the ice-cream parlor."

They came out of the stables and turned onto the street where they had parked the car.

"Just because you city slickers don't appreciate us Western dudes," Lisa began, then she stopped, stepping back nervously as she almost bumped into a tall man standing by the gate.

"Pardon me, ma'am," he said in a deep, drawling voice.

Lisa and the girls stared at him. He was middle-aged and good-looking in a lean, rugged sort of way. He was wearing cowboy boots and a big black Western hat.

The man touched his hat like a cowboy from an old movie. "I hope you won't be offended if I talk to you, seeing that I'm a complete stranger, but I just happened to be driving past and I saw the horses through the fence. That was the last thing I expected to see in the middle of Detroit city, so I just had to stop and take a look. I saw you taking that jump, ma'am. That was a fine piece of riding—a mighty fine piece of riding, if you don't mind my saying so."

"Why, thank you," Lisa said sweetly. "I wasn't at my best today, but the horse was playing up. You know how it is."

"Mom!" Tia muttered under her breath, digging her mother in the side. She knew how easily Lisa could get carried away.

"You're not from around these parts, I take it," the man said.

"Yes, she is," Tia said quickly, before Lisa could start talking about the Pony Express or the plains of Africa. "We live right here in Detroit."

"But I did grow up in the South," Lisa said. "That's where I got my love of horses—back on the range. . . ."

"The only range she's been near is in the kitchen, and it's electric," Tamera whispered to Tia, making Tia smile.

The man obviously hadn't heard. He was smiling at Lisa. "That explains it then," the man said. "No city woman could ever learn to ride like that. It's only back home that women are born to ride."

"So you're not from around here then, Mr. . . . uh?"

The man tipped his hat again. "Ronald Hunter of Buckeye, Texas, at your service, ma'am," he said. "Everyone calls me Tex. I'm just in town for a few days—up attending the farm-machinery convention. I'm looking to buy a new hay baler."

"Yeah, they do seem to wear out quickly these days," Lisa said. "They don't make machinery like they used to."

Tia and Tamera exchanged another despairing glance.

"And might I be so bold as to ask your name?" Tex asked.

"You sure can, Mr. Hunter," Lisa said, sounding like a cross between Scarlett O'Hara and Calamity Jane. "I'm Lisa Landry—Ms. Lisa Landry, and this is my daughter, Tia, and her sister, Tamera."

"Mighty pleased to meet you, ma'am, and you, too, ladies," Tex said, beaming at them. "The big city is an awful lonely place, and I didn't think I'd meet my own type of person while I was here. You come here to ride the horses a lot, I take it?"

"This is the first time since last October," Tia said quickly, before Lisa could claim that they owned the stables or were in training for the Olympics.

"The weather's so bad in Detroit in the winter," Lisa added. "They close up the riding schools for those months. We're just out here enjoying the spring sunshine and getting back in the saddle."

The man looked away down the street as if he was

thinking. Then he glanced at his watch and said, "I'm afraid I have to get back for a four o'clock appointment at the convention, but I was wondering if you would do me the honor of having dinner with me tonight. I don't know any of the good places to eat here, and it's no fun eating alone, however fancy the restaurant is."

"I'd be delighted," Lisa said.

"That's really good of you, Ms. Landry. I really appreciate it," Tex said. "And maybe you'd know a good place to eat? Not one of these fancy modern places where they give you a tiny dollop of raw fish and some undercooked vegetables. I like real food—a good thick steak I can sink my teeth into—know what I mean?"

"I sure do," Lisa said, "and I know just the place."

"Terrific," Tex said. "Could you give me your address so I can send a taxi to pick you up at your door? It's not right for a lady to be out alone in the city at night."

"Why, certainly, Mr. Hunter," Lisa said in a syrupy voice. She rattled off their address and they agreed on a time.

"Until seven then, ma'am," Tex said, tipping his hat yet again.

The girls waited until they had reached their car and Tex had vanished in the other direction, then they both turned on Lisa at once.

"Have you gone totally crazy, Mom?" Tia demanded. "You've agreed to go out with a complete stranger. You never let guys pick you up on the street."

"This is different," Lisa said. "He didn't pick me up on the street. It was at the riding stables, and Mr. Hunter is a Texan visitor. And I've only said I'll go to dinner with him. And he seems like a perfect gentleman. Did you notice the way he tipped his hat and called me ma'am. And did you see how he didn't want me out alone on the city streets? He's sending a taxi for me! He really knows how to treat a woman. You don't find guys like that in Detroit."

"But he could be a complete phony, Lisa," Tamera said.

"I don't think so," Lisa said. "He looked like a genuine cowboy to me. Those boots looked like the real thing."

"I hope you're right," Tia said. "I worry about you, Mom."

"We're only going to dinner," Lisa said, defending herself. "What could happen to me at a restaurant?"

"And what is this famous steak restaurant you were telling him about?" Tia went on. "I didn't think you liked steak. You never eat at steak restaurants."

"I'll tell you the answer to that just as soon as I look it up in the Yellow Pages," Lisa said with a knowing smile.

Later that evening, Tia and Tamera lay on their beds, watching TV.

"It's eleven o'clock," Tia said. "She should be home by now. I hope she's okay."

"She'll be fine," Tamera said. "If anyone can take care of herself, it's your mother."

"I should have given her a curfew," Tia said. "I should have told that Tex guy that she had to be home by ten. I just hope he doesn't try to get fresh with her in the taxi."

Tamera started laughing. "Just listen to yourself," she said. "You sound like the mother, not the daughter."

"Someone has to look after her," Tia said. "If she's not back soon, she's grounded."

"Tia, it's only eleven o'clock. You're allowed out this late at weekends."

"Yeah, but I'm with boys I know, not complete strangers who picked me up outside the riding stables." She rolled over and leaned close to Tamera. "Tell me the truth—have you ever heard of a black cowboy?"

"I guess there have to be black cowboys," Tamera said. "Why not?"

"Have you ever seen any on a TV show?" Tia said. "The only black cowboys I know play wide receiver for Dallas, and this guy is too old for that."

"You really think he's a phony?" Tamera asked, also looking worried now.

"He could be."

"Why would anyone go around pretending to be a cowboy?"

Tia shrugged. "How should I know?" she said. "There are some weird people in the world."

"Tia, your mom isn't entirely stupid," Tamera

said. "And she certainly has street smarts. She wouldn't let any guy con her."

Tia jumped up. "Listen, isn't that a taxi?" She ran across to the window. "Yes, there she is now. What's keeping her so long? Why doesn't she get out? I hope that old guy doesn't expect a good-night kiss!"

Just then they saw Lisa get out of the taxi. The door slammed behind her and she came up the front path. Tia sprinted down the stairs to meet her.

"Hi, baby," Lisa called excitedly. "Did you wait up for me? That was so sweet."

Tia stood on the stairs with her hands on her hips. "Just where have you been, young lady?" she demanded. "Do you know what time it is?"

Lisa giggled. "Good imitation. Sounds just like me."

"I'm serious, Mom," Tia said. "This isn't a laughing matter. It's past eleven o'clock, and I was worried about you."

"Why? I only went out to dinner."

"With a complete stranger. Dinners aren't supposed to last this long."

"So I showed him the sights of Detroit afterward. We went for a walk along the lakefront." She stopped and sighed happily. "I had the best time, Tia. Tex is a wonderful person—so kind and considerate. He made me feel like a princess." She sank onto the nearest sofa. "He told me all about his ranch in Texas. He owns this huge spread, Tia. Thousands and thousands of cows, or cattle, or whatever they call them. And he built it all up from nothing. Now he's a millionaire."

"And you believed that?" Tia demanded.

"Why shouldn't I believe it?" Lisa said angrily. "He's staying at the best hotel in town, and he didn't worry what we spent on dinner. And he's not married."

"Divorced?" Tia asked.

"Never been married," Lisa said. "When he was young he was in the military, then in agricultural college, then he was trying to build up the ranch. He said he had no money to take girls out in those days. Now the ranch keeps him too busy to meet people." She leaned back and closed her eyes. "It must have been fate that brought us together today. If I hadn't been determined to learn to ride . . ."

"Mom, I know what you're like. When you want to make a good impression, you do sometimes stretch the truth a little," Tia said kindly.

"It wasn't my fault that he seemed to think I was a country girl who knew all about riding horses and roping cows," Lisa said. "It would have been dumb of me to tell him that I'd never seen a live cow close up, except at a rodeo."

"That was a live bull, Mom. There's a big difference," Tia said dryly.

Lisa shrugged. "They both have horns and say moo," she said. "That's good enough for me. And anyway, there will be time later to tell Tex the truth about me."

"Later?"

"He wants to see me again, tomorrow," Lisa said. "And he's staying on a couple of days after the convention ends. He told me he has the feeling that I'm the woman he's been looking for all his life."

Tia went over to the sofa and sat on the arm beside her mother. "Mom, be careful, won't you," she said. "You've only just met him. You don't know a thing about him."

"I know all that I want to know," Lisa said. "I have a feeling about this, baby. I think I've just met Mr. Right!"

Chapter 3

"How come there are no free tables in this whole cafeteria?" The twins' friend Sarah demanded as she stood clutching her tray while students jostled past her.

Right behind her, Tia and Tamera also tried to stop their trays from getting knocked over as they battled their way through the crush.

"I swear this cafeteria gets more crowded every day," Michelle complained, coming up to join them. "Hey, watch it, buster," she snapped as a boy pushed past her, fighting to get to a table.

"Look, someone's leaving in the corner," Tamera said. The girls sprinted across the cafeteria, not caring whom they mowed down with their trays, and flung themselves at the table at the same time as a small skinny boy.

"I got here first," the boy said fiercely.

Tamera put down her tray, prepared to do battle, and then she saw who it was. It was their pint-size neighbor, Roger, who was constantly hanging around and bugging them. He had never learned to take no for an answer and still believed that he could make one of the twins fall in love with him.

"Beat it, Roger," Tamera said.

"Hey, I got here first," Roger insisted. "Duane told me to save a table for him, and he'll beat me to a pulp if I don't."

Tia put down her tray beside Tamera's. "Roger, who would you rather face—one mean Duane or a whole table full of angry and very hungry girls?"

Roger looked alarmed as Sarah, then Michelle, then Chantal and Denise all put their trays on the table.

"Don't make me go back to Duane," Roger said, looking as if he was about to burst into tears. Then his expression brightened. "I could stay and keep you company," he suggested. "I'm small. I could squeeze in between Tia and Tamera."

"Not in your wildest dreams, Roger," Tamera said. "Go on, beat it."

"You don't deserve me as your homey," Roger shot over his shoulder as he moved away. "One day you'll push me too far and I'll find another girl to shower my affection on."

"Roll on that day!" Tamera called after him.

Tia smiled as she watched him go. "Poor Roger. Everyone always puts him down," she said.

"Poor Roger can look after himself," Tamera said.

"I hope you remember that he blackmailed us into going to a dance with him once? I don't trust that guy further than I can throw him."

"This place is like a zoo today. What is happening here?" Michelle asked, smoothing her hair as she sat down. "Where do all these kids come from? They can't all go to our school."

"Principal Vernon said the school was getting overcrowded," Sarah said.

"Someone can have my place in math class," Tamera said quickly. "But I'm not giving up my seat in the cafeteria."

"I think I'll drop out and become a hermit," Sarah said with a sigh. "A cave or a mountaintop . . . the wide-open spaces sound pretty good right now."

"She should go stay with Tex on his ranch," Tamera muttered to Tia. "I bet he's got enough wide-open spaces for anyone."

Tia gave her a look that made her suppress a giggle.

"I've had enough of school," Chantal said. "It seems like this quarter has gone on forever and ever. How long is it to spring break?"

"Three weeks," Tamera said. "I've been counting the days."

"That's right!" Denise said excitedly. "You get to go to Disney World, you lucky thing."

"And I get to go with her," Tia said. "And my mom, too. I'll have to talk to her about some major shopping pretty soon. I don't have a single thing in my wardrobe that's right for Disney World."

"Your mom's in such a great mood right now, she'll probably give you a hundred bucks and tell you to go enjoy yourself," Tamera suggested. "Or maybe Tex will give you a blank check—or his charge card."

"Tex? Is that the cowboy guy you told us about? Is he still around?" Sarah asked.

Tia sighed. "Yeah. He's stayed on a whole extra week, and it doesn't look like he's planning on leaving either. He's taken my mom out every single night so far."

"She must really like him," Denise said.

"She's crazy about him," Tia said gloomily. "Everything she says is Tex this and Tex that."

"And he's really a millionaire?"

"So my mom says," Tia said. "He's brought her some great presents and sends taxis to pick her up when he can't get there himself."

"Ooh, Tia. You might be getting a rich stepfather. Wouldn't that be cool?" Chantal said excitedly.

Tia shook her head. "It would be terrible," she said. "You haven't seen him. He's like a cartoon cowboy. He tips his hat and says, 'Yes, ma'am.' He's totally wrong for my mother. I just hope she's smart enough to see it."

"If she marries him, will you guys have to go live on the ranch in Texas?" Denise asked.

"Can you see Lisa living on a ranch?" Tamera giggled.

"It's not funny, Tamera," Tia snapped. "Don't you see? If my mother marries this guy, then I'll have to move away from here—away from my friends and my school and away from you."

Tamera's face grew solemn. "Yeah, I guess so," she said. Then she shook her head. "But it won't happen. Lisa is a total city person. There's no way she'd go live on a ranch in the boonies. She just likes all the attention this guy is giving her." She reached across and touched Tia's hand. "Don't worry. We'll find her a cool new guy at Disney World and make her forget all about Tex."

"I hope you're right," Tia said. "Because there's no way I'm leaving here and leaving you!"

"Tia, your mom is a fun-loving person," Tamera said. "She must be getting fed up with a boring old cowboy by now. I mean, the guy is so completely not with it, isn't he? Did you hear last night when your mom asked him if he liked Spike Lee, and he said he'd never tried it, but if she wanted to cook some, it was fine with him."

The other girls all burst out laughing. Tia tried to smile too, but her insides were tying themselves in knots. She can't be falling in love with Tex, she told herself. She couldn't expect me to leave Tamera and move away to Texas. Not now, just when I feel like I belong here!

"Okay, as soon as we get home, we make Disney World shopping lists," Tamera said as they got off the bus. "Shorts, lots of shorts, don't you think? We don't want sun dresses in case they fly up on the scary rides." She linked her arm through Tia's. "You will come on all the scary rides with me, won't you? I don't want my dad to know that I'm too chicken to go on them alone."

"Uh, sure," Tia said. "Whatever you say."

Tamera looked at her sharply. "What's with you?" she asked. "Aren't you looking forward to going to Disney World?"

"Of course," Tia said. "I just can't stop worrying about my mother and Tex."

"He has to go back to his ranch sometime soon," Tamera said. "Don't the cows need milking or something? And when he's gone, she'll wonder what she saw in him. She'll come to Disney World and have a great time, and everything will be back to normal."

"I hope you're right," Tia said.

She opened the front door.

Lisa leaped up from the sofa, where she had been sitting. "Honey, we need to do some serious shopping!" she yelled, flinging herself at Tia.

"For Disney World—all right!" Tia exclaimed, her face lighting up.

"Oh, Disney World," Lisa said. "That's right. I'd forgotten all about it. Oh well, too bad. Never mind. Tex can fly you to Disney World any old time you want."

Tia walked around her mother, looking at her as if she had turned into a dangerous animal. "Too bad? Never mind? Are you saying that we're not going to Disney World?"

Lisa laughed nervously. "I'm sorry, sugar. It just totally slipped my mind."

"How can something as totally awesome as Disney World slip your mind?" Tia yelled.

"I was concentrating so hard on what Tex was saying. I wanted to make sure I hadn't misunderstood when he said he wanted me to come see what the ranch was like and whether I could be happy there for the rest of my life."

Tia stood there with her mouth open. "Tex asked you to marry him?" She tried not to look too disgusted.

Lisa shrugged. "That's what it sounded like to me. He said it wasn't fair for me to make up my mind before I'd had a chance to see for myself. And you, too, honeybun. He wanted us both to know that we'd be happy on the ranch. So he invited us down there, and I said it would have to be when you were out of school during spring break."

"I'm going to a ranch in Texas instead of Disney World?" Tia yelled. "Mom, you can't do this to me." She turned to her sister. "Tell her, Tamera. Tell her she can't do this to me."

"Disney World won't be any fun if Tia's not there, Lisa," Tamera said.

"Do you know how much I was looking forward to that Disney World trip, Mom?" Tia demanded. "Okay, if you want to go to the ranch, you go, but let me go to Disney World with Tamera."

"But I have to know that you're going to be happy, too, Tia," Lisa said.

"How can I be happy on a crummy ranch?" Tia

snapped. "What am I going to do—talk to the cows all day?"

"It's a million-dollar spread, and Tex has his own plane and you can be in Dallas in twenty minutes," Lisa said.

"Whoopdeedoo," Tia said flatly.

Lisa took her shoulders and gazed at her daughter steadily. "Tia, it's my life we're talking about here. Tex is a wonderful man. He wants to marry me. He wants to take care of me. We'll never have to worry about money again. Are you trying to tell me I should forget about him because you want to go to Disney World?"

Tia shrugged and tried to break free. "Leave me alone," she said.

"Tia, think about it. You'd have a father. Isn't that what you've always wanted—your own father to come root for you at school and boast about how smart you are?"

"I've already got Ray," Tia said. "He does all that."

"Honey, Ray isn't your father, and he never will be," Lisa said.

"But I like living here with Ray, and I'm not leaving Tamera," Tia said, finally shaking herself loose. "I don't want to go to Texas. I don't want to go anywhere."

She ran upstairs and flung herself down, crying on her bed.

Lisa looked at Tamera. "Can you talk to her, Tamera?" she asked. "Can you make her understand? I only want the best for her, too—I want her to go to the best college and have a great life. If I married Tex, she could do all that."

Tamera stared at her. "You're asking me to persuade my own sister to move away after I've found her again?" she said. "I want the best for you, Lisa, but not if it means losing Tia."

Lisa stood there for a moment, then she followed Tia up the stairs. Tia was lying on her bed, just staring at the ceiling.

Lisa knocked on the door and then came into the room. "Can I come in?" she asked.

Tia still stared at the ceiling. "You can do what you want. You're the mother. You get to call the shots," she said. "All I have to do is get dragged along wherever you want to go. I don't matter at all."

"Of course you matter, sugar," Lisa said, sitting down cautiously on the edge of Tia's bed. "I'm doing this for both of us. This might be the chance of our lifetimes. When have I ever met a man like Tex before? You'd get to go to the best college, and I'd be queen of the ranch. That doesn't sound so bad, does it?"

Tia turned to look at her mother. "Mom, do you really see yourself as queen of the ranch? Give me a break."

"I could learn," Lisa said. "I love horses. I might learn to love the wide-open spaces." Then she reached across and took Tia's hand. "We both knew this couldn't go on forever, didn't we? Living here with Ray and Tamera, I mean. It was only to give you two girls a chance to know each other again. It wasn't meant to be permanent."

"I don't see why not," Tia said. "We were all getting along great."

"But the time had to come when Ray or I met that special person we'd been looking for," Lisa said. "I thought once that maybe Ray and I . . . but that was stupid. We're complete opposites in every way."

"So are you and Tex," Tia said.

"But Tex worships the ground I tread on," Lisa said. "Ray doesn't. In fact, he'd prefer it if I didn't tread on his ground at all. It will be better for all of us if we move out. Ray can get on with his life and meet someone new, and you and Tamera can see each other during vacations. Tex will fly her down to the ranch."

"Sure—vacations. That sounds great," Tia said. "What about the rest of the year, when we need each other? When we meet, it will be like we're strangers all over again."

"What if Ray had met someone and fallen in love?" Lisa demanded. "We'd have had to move out then."

"But not out of state. We could have moved a block away, and Tamera and I could have seen each other all day at school. This is goodbye forever."

"Please give it a try, Tia," Lisa said. "Maybe it won't work out. Maybe I'll decide that Tex and his life aren't right for me, but I've got to give it a try. I'm just asking you to be open-minded until you've tried it. Two weeks of your life aren't much to give up for me, are they?"

Tia sat up. "Two weeks? I thought we were going for spring vacation."

"Tex suggested you come down a few days early so that you can go to school with the local kids to see what it's like."

"You want me to take time off from school?" Tia said.

"Only a few days," Lisa said.

"Mom, what if I miss something important in math? I can't afford to take days off. I'm sure Principal Vernon will agree with me."

"I've already asked your principal and he said okay," Lisa said, turning her back so that she couldn't see Tia's angry face. "It's all settled, Tia. We're going down to Texas whether you like it or not!"

"Are you okay?" Tamera asked gently as she came into the bedroom and saw Tia standing, staring out of the window.

"I can't believe it," Tia said in a choked voice. "In two weeks' time, I might never see any of this again."

"Two weeks?" Tamera asked. "You're leaving before spring break?"

"Yeah. I get to miss a week of school. I'm really mad about it, Tamera. We're learning so much new stuff in math. I might miss something important."

"You're upset about missing a week of math?" Tamera said, wrinkling her nose. "Sometimes I wonder if you're really my sister after all. I'd do anything to get out of math for a week." Then her face lit up. "Hey, I've got a great idea. We could do one of our famous switcheroos. I could take your place. Tex would never know the difference."

"But what about Disney World?" Tia asked.

"Oh yeah, I'd forgotten about Disney World," Tamera said. "I'd do a lot for you, but not miss my one chance to go to Disney World with my dad. Sorry about that."

"It's okay. The old switcheroo wouldn't have worked this time anyway. My mom would know it wasn't me, and I guess she's right. I do have to give this a chance, I suppose. If she really is in love with this guy, I couldn't be selfish and stand in her way. It might be her one chance for happiness." She turned to look at Tamera. "I just can't believe that I won't see you again!"

"Hey, it's not like you're going to jail or to live in Australia," Tamera said, trying to sound upbeat. "Maybe Tex will give you your own plane and you can fly back to see me on weekends."

"Yeah, right," Tia said bitterly. She turned to look at her sister. "Do you really think he's that rich? It all sounds too good to be true to me. I just hope he hasn't lied to my mother."

"We'll soon find out, won't we?" Tamera said. "Either way, it's a win-win situation. If he's stinking rich, you'll be able to live the lifestyles of the rich and famous, and that wouldn't be so bad, would it? Spring in Paris, winter in Australia, your own plane . . . if he's lied, your mom will decide he's a no-good creep and you'll come home again."

"I hope he's been lying," Tia said. "I know it will hurt my mom and she'll be mad for a while, but I'm sure she'll come around to seeing that she belongs here."

"You might like it there," Tamera said. "You might have a really great time."

"I don't see how without you," Tia said. "All of my great times have been with you, Tamera."

"Don't start talking like that or you'll make me cry," Tamera said. "And you know how I hate crying. It makes my mascara run."

"But it's true," Tia said. "My life only started to be fun after I met you. We've been through a lot together."

"Yeah, sure," Tamera said with a grin. "Working at Rocket Burger, dragging you out of that fire in the locker room, sharing Roger as our dance date . . ."

"I was thinking of the good times, not the nightmares," Tia said. "Like last Christmas with all the family. It was the first time in my whole life that I knew what it felt like to belong to a family."

"Me, too," Tamera said. "It was great, wasn't it?"

"And now we'll never do it again." Tia sighed. "Next Christmas I'll be on the ranch saying 'Heehaw' and getting a new rope and branding iron in my stocking."

Tamera put her arm around her sister's shoulder. "You might spend Christmas in London or Paris, and you could ask to take your sister with you."

Tia made a face. "Tex might be rich, but somehow I don't see him in Paris, do you? He felt out of place in Detroit."

"We'll work it out somehow," Tamera said. "We're like the post office—neither rain, nor hail, nor sleet, nor snow is going to keep us apart. They won't keep me away from you, even if I have to mail myself to you in a package or sneak onto the ranch, disguised as a cow!"

Tia threw her arms around Tamera's neck. "You're the greatest," she said.

"I'll remember that the next time I want to borrow your best sweater," Tamera said. Then she smiled as she remembered what Lisa had said. "At least you'll get some new clothes out of this. Your mom said she wanted to take you for major shopping. Go for it."

Tia walked away from the window and sat down on the bed. "Somehow the thought of new jeans and checked shirts and bandannas doesn't excite me," she said.

"They have formal occasions out in the boonies," Tamera said. "You'll need one of those full square-dancing skirts and a lacy blouse, too."

"Shut up," Tia said, half laughing. "They don't really do stuff like that anymore, do they? They have to have real dances to real music. . . . They have to have TV. . . . Tell me they have TV, Tamera. I might not even survive two weeks down there."

"Then your mom won't survive either," Tamera said. "She can't exist without her soap operas."

"Idea number one," Tia said, pretending to jot

something down in a book. "Hide the TV, if there is one." She shot Tamera a worried look. "Ohmy-gosh, do you think there's electricity? Do you think we'll have to get water from the well?"

"He's rich, Tia. He can afford electricity, I'm sure," Tamera said.

Tia started to pace up and down. "I just wish I could get this all over with. I don't think I can wait two weeks until I find out my fate."

Chapter 4

"You have to help me pack," Tia said to Tamera, looking up at her sister from an empty suitcase on her bed. The rest of the bed was invisible under mountains of clothing. "I have no idea what to take to the boonies. I have no idea what to wear to a hoedown. . . . I don't even know what a hoedown is!"

"Simple—it's the opposite of a hoe-up," Tamera said brightly. She was trying hard to stay upbeat for Tia's sake. She knew how hard this must be for Tia. It was hard enough for herself, knowing that this might be the beginning of the end for them.

She picked up a pile of Tia's clothes. "At least you got a lot of good new stuff out of this," she said.

"Yeah, but nothing fun, like you got for Disney World," Tia said.

"You can take some of my Disney World stuff if you want," Tamera said quickly.

"Thanks, but can you see their faces in Texas if I wore that halter top you bought? I bet they don't allow their women to expose their shoulders." She looked up worriedly. "Do you think I should take some hats? Do you think they still wear bonnets?"

Tamera laughed. "Tia, you're not traveling back in time, you're just going to another state. It's not *Little House on the Prairie.* It will be just like here, only hotter and drier and with more cows." She looked critically at Tia's pile of new clothing. "You didn't get any new jeans," she said.

"I refuse to wear new jeans, even for Texas," Tia said. "I'm taking my favorite pair with all the rips in the knees. I have to show them I'm the big-city girl and I know how to be cool. But I should take these Levi's, too, shouldn't I—in case I have to ride horses. I don't want my favorite jeans to smell of horse forever."

"I thought your mom bought you some real riding pants."

"She did," Tia said. "She bought me a whole riding outfit with the hat and everything. I look like a total geek in them. I look like an English princess about to take riding lessons at the palace."

Tamera nodded. "I saw your mom in her new Western riding outfit. Scary. You have to make her tone down this 'born and bred among the horses' act, Tia. She's going to end up looking like a fool when Tex finds out she can't ride."

Tia shrugged. "She's been taking riding lessons every day this week, and she says she's got the hang of it now. And besides, you know my mom. She figures that she can put off telling him the truth for as long as possible—hopefully until they are married. But I'll do my best to keep her in line, although it won't be easy."

She started piling clothes into the suitcase, not really seeming to care what she was taking. When the case could hold no more, she crammed it shut. "There. That should do it. That's enough clothes for two weeks, isn't it?'

Tamera nodded again. "Plenty, especially since I don't imagine the entertainment scene is exactly wild out there. I can't see you heading to the nearest coffee house."

"I imagine the nearest coffee house is in Dallas, a hundred miles away. I'm taking all my schoolbooks with me so that I can get ahead on my reading."

"Exactly what I would have done," Tamera quipped.

Tia looked up at her fondly. "I wish you were coming," she said. "I think I could stand anything if you were there with me."

"I wish you were coming to Disney World," Tamera said. "It won't be the same without you. Now I'll never go on Space Mountain. There's no way I'm grabbing my dad's hand on a roller coaster and letting him know that I'm scared."

"I'll call you every day and let you know how it's going," Tia said at the very same moment as Tamera said, "Call me every day and let me know how it's going."

They looked at each other and laughed.

"Maybe I won't need to call you," Tia said. "We've got twin telepathy, remember?"

"Right," Tamera said. "Do you think it works long distance?"

"Sure, why not?"

"That will save on the phone bills," Tamera said.

"But just in case, don't forget to give me your number at Disney World," Tia said softly.

"And don't forget to leave me your number at the ranch."

"It's on the refrigerator already." Tia looked around the room. "I love this room. I can't believe I might not be sharing it with you any longer."

"You won't have to fight me for the bathroom," Tamera said. She slid her arm around Tia's shoulder. "It's only for two weeks," she said. "Even if your mom does decide to marry Tex, you'd come back here again for a while, while she gets ready for the wedding. And you can tell her it's harmful to your education to move you in the middle of a school year. So at least you can stay until summer."

"Yeah, sure," Tia said bleakly.

Tamera hugged her. "And it might never happen, Tia. Lisa might take one look and yell, 'Get me out of this joint,' and you'll be on your way home again."

"I wish," Tia said. "Tamera, am I really being selfish, wishing that my mom and Tex don't hit it off?"

"Of course not. You and I both think he's totally wrong for her. So we're only really thinking of her, too."

"Yeah," Tia said, looking slightly more hopeful.

"Come on, we don't want to waste your last night here," Tamera said. "Let's go down to the Rocket Burger and see if any of our friends are there. My treat."

"Now I really know I'm leaving," Tia said, brushing back tears. "You've never offered to treat me before."

"I just want you to remember me fondly," Tamera said, "Oh, and Tia. If you don't come back, can I have your CD collection and your history notes?"

"Get outta here," Tia said, laughing as she chased Tamera down the stairs.

Next morning the taxi arrived to take Lisa and Tia to the airport. The taxi driver looked horrified at the mountain of luggage Lisa wanted to cram into the trunk.

"Are you going away for a year, lady?" he asked. "This is a taxi, not a moving van."

"I'm just taking the essentials that one needs at a millionaire's ranch," Lisa said as she climbed into the backseat. "Did I mention that we're talking about my future husband, the millionaire, who owns one of the biggest ranches in Texas?"

"Yeah, and I'm really Denzel Washington in disguise," the taxi driver growled as he got into the driver's seat.

"Stupid man," Lisa muttered. Tia and Tamera exchanged a grin.

"Well, this is it, I guess," Tia said, giving Tamera a hug. She climbed into the taxi beside her mother. "Bye. I'll miss you."

"I'll miss you, too," Tamera said. "Hope you have fun."

The taxi backed out of the driveway.

"See you in two weeks," Tamera yelled as they drove off.

"Have a great time at Disney World," Tia yelled back.

Then they were gone.

Tamera waved until the taxi turned the corner and disappeared.

Ray put an arm around his daughter's shoulder. "Come into the house, honey. You don't have a jacket on."

"She's gone, Dad," Tamera said, her voice choking. "I can't believe it might be forever."

"She'll be back in two weeks, Tamera," Ray said brightly.

"But after that . . . she might move to Texas forever, and I'll never see her again."

"You knew this might happen someday, Tamera," Ray said. "Lisa's a very attractive woman. She was bound to meet the right man someday and want to marry him."

"Why couldn't you have been the right man?" Tamera demanded.

"Me?" Ray gave a nervous laugh. "The right man

for Lisa? Give me a break, Tamera. We can't stand each other."

"Yes you can. You fight a lot, but secretly you like each other. I know it."

"I don't know what gave you that idea," Ray said. "Lisa and I are exact opposites. She's loud and uncouth, I'm sophisticated and very . . ."

"Couth?" Tamera finished for him.

"And her taste in guys leaves a lot to be desired," Ray said. "If she prefers this cowboy type to a cultured man-about-town . . ."

"See, that proves it," Tamera said delightedly. "You always run down the guys she dates. That proves that secretly you're jealous of them."

"It does not. I've never heard of anything so stupid," Ray said. "And even though I'm very fond of Tia and I want you girls to be happy, there is no way I'd marry Lisa just to keep her here, even if she'd have me, which she wouldn't. Case closed."

"Okay, Dad. Keep your hair on," Tamera said, grinning at his embarrassed face. Then she remembered that this wasn't a joke—it was deadly serious and she might be losing Tia forever. "Besides, it's too late," she added bleakly. "Lisa's already heading to Texas to become Mrs. Cowboy—and I'm never going to see my sister again!"

Chapter 5

"I wonder which is Tex's private plane?" Lisa asked Tia excitedly as they deplaned into the terminal at Dallas. "Do you think it's that Learjet over there? Nah, maybe that's a little too fancy, but you never know." She was already looking around. "I don't see him. Do you think he's waiting down at the baggage-claim area?"

Hope surged up inside Tia. He's not here. He's chickened out. We can go home again!

"Ms. Landry?" Someone tapped Lisa on the arm. It was a stocky man wearing a cowboy hat.

"Yes? What do you want?" Lisa asked nervously.

"Mr. Hunter sent me to get you, ma'am," he said. "I'm Jose, his ranch manager."

"What happened to Mr. Hunter?"

Tia could hear the tension in her mother's voice.

"He was planning to come himself, but he had a difficult calving—one of his best animals—and he didn't want to leave it. So he asked me to come get you and say he's sorry he's not here himself."

"That's okay," Lisa said. "We'll be with him in half an hour, won't we?"

"More like two and a half hours, ma'am," Jose said.

"What about the private plane?"

"The plane's in the shop for its annual maintenance," Jose said. "And besides, I don't fly planes. The station wagon's outside."

"Hear that, Mom? The station wagon's outside," Tia said, trying not to smile. She was feeling more hopeful by the minute. Tex wasn't a millionaire at all. He was just one big phony. Lisa was going to be disappointed and mad and want to go straight home again. Tia grinned to herself as she followed her mother down to the baggage-claim area and then out to the parking lot.

The station wagon turned out to be a new Jeep Grand Cherokee. Okay, so he has a nice car, Tia thought to herself. Lots of people had nice cars. Ray had a nice car. That didn't make him a millionaire.

Jose turned on the air conditioning as they drove out of the airport and then headed into the flat, dry landscape beyond. At first there were suburbs and patches of green. As they drove farther, the green disappeared to be replaced by golden brown scrubland stretching as far as the eye could see. Nothing broke the monotony apart from occasional barbed-wire fences or windmills. It was the most boring country that Tia had ever seen.

No shopping malls or restaurants or movie theaters—in fact, a hundred miles of nothing! Tia thought. I bet my mother is already deciding that she's made a mistake.

"So, when do we get to Tex's land?" Lisa asked after they had driven for a while. "I don't want to be dozing when we get there."

"We've already been on his land for the past half hour," Jose said. "All this on the right belongs to the Bar T. That's the name of his ranch, on account of the boss's name being Tex. And those animals on the skyline—they're all his."

"Wow, I mean that's fascinating," Lisa said. "Isn't it fascinating, Tia honey?"

"Oh yeah, sure," Tia said. "Fascinating."

"How far to the nearest town?" she asked.

"There's a store and a school and a couple of churches in Buckeye," Jose said. "But I wouldn't call it a real town. Closest real town is Fort Worth or Dallas."

"I'm glad I brought all those books with me," Tia said.

"Here we are," Jose said. He swung onto a dirt road. They bounced along for a while before they drove under a wooden gateway with a carved sign over it: Bar T Ranch. Prize Texas Longhorns.

"Prize Texas Longhorns," Lisa said. "I guess they must be cows."

"Cattle, ma'am," Jose said.

"Holy cow—I mean cattle!" Lisa exclaimed as they came around a bend and the ranch house appeared before them. Tia took one look and knew that Tex hadn't been lying after all. This was definitely a millionaire's house. It was a long, low ranch house with a porch running the full length of it, and it was huge. It was shaded by two big trees, and off to one side, several fine-looking horses trotted nervously around a corral. It looked to Tia just like a movie set for an old-time Western.

Tex came running out at the sound of the car, two big dogs at his heels.

"Lisa, I'm so sorry," he said as he opened the door and helped her down. "I just couldn't risk losing one of my best cows. I do hope you understand." He stood there, looking at Lisa. "It's just wonderful that you're here," he said. Then he wrenched his gaze away. "And little Tia, too."

"I'm no smaller than she is," Tia said.

Tex forced a fake smile. "Isn't she adorable," he said. "Come on into the house. I'll have Maria fix us a nice cold jug of iced tea and something to eat."

He strode ahead with Lisa, leaving Jose to bring in the bags. Tia followed, already feeling like a piece of left luggage herself. The dogs sniffed at her, then wagged their tails and licked her as she petted them. She realized that in her whole life she had never owned a dog. She could hear her mother exclaiming to Tex how wonderful everything was and how happy she was to be with him again.

It was cool inside the house. The main living room

was long and open, with tiled floor and low leather sofas. On the wall was a giant pair of cow's horns, and there were pieces of Indian pottery and carvings on the shelf that ran around the walls.

"I hope you've forgiven me for not coming to meet you," Tex said to Lisa. "I hope this will make up for it." He handed her a little box.

"Holy— I mean, this is beautiful, Tex," Lisa said. She held up a bracelet that sparkled with real diamonds. "Thank you so much. You are the sweetest guy in the whole world." She reached up to kiss him on his cheek.

"And I didn't want you to feel left out, little Tia." Tex handed her a box. Inside was a gold bracelet with horse charms on it.

"Thank you, it's lovely," Tia said, stepping back so that she didn't have to kiss him, too. She was thinking that she would probably have loved it when she was about twelve and if anyone other than Tex had given it to her.

"Come on, Tia, let me show you your room," Tex said. "I had Maria fix it up for you. She knows what young girls like better than I do." Tia and Lisa followed him down a cool tiled hallway. The dogs stayed close to Tia. They had already decided she was a new friend. The touch of their warm soft fur against her legs was reassuring.

The room was at the far end of the house, and it really was a dream room—white lacy curtains at the windows, white lace comforter on the bed, and a ruffle around the vanity. There was a wicker sofa to curl up on, and a small desk and her own TV and CD player.

"I wouldn't want you to get bored while you're here," Tex said. "At least you'll have something to do until you make friends."

"Wow! Th-thanks," Tia stammered.

"And after we've had a bite to eat, I'll introduce you to your horses. I've found a feisty little mare for you, Lisa, and a real pretty little filly for Tia. And when it comes to vehicles, the keys are hanging up in the hallway. Just help yourself when you feel like driving somewhere, Tia."

"I can't drive yet," Tia said.

"Can't drive yet?" Tex laughed. "Kids around here drive as soon as they can walk."

"'But what about a license? I'm not old enough yet."

"Sure you are. We'll just get you a license to drive farm vehicles. That's what all the kids have. I'll give you some lessons, and then you can get some practice with my little pickup truck. If you like it, it's yours." He smiled broadly at her, then turned to Lisa. "And now, let me show you your room. I think you're going to love it."

They moved away down the hall, leaving Tia looking around her. It really was the prettiest room she had ever had in her life. My own TV, she thought. She wouldn't have to fight with Tamera over the Discovery Channel versus MTV. She opened the door at the back of the room and found her own bathroom, complete with fluffy white towels and a blue marble tub. If Tamera could see me now, she'd freak, Tia thought. She wanted to call her right away and noticed that there was a phone on her desk. Tex really had thought of everything possible to make her happy.

Maybe I was being selfish and hasty about this, she thought. I was determined to hate it here, but maybe it won't be so bad after all. . . .

"Hi, it's me," Tia said as Tamera picked up the phone. "I've been trying to call for hours. Where have you been?"

"Out with my dad. He took me out to a movie to try to cheer me up. How is it?"

"You won't believe it—it's incredible, Tamera. I have a huge room with everything you could possibly want in it—it's so pretty, like something out of a magazine, and I have my own horse, and Tex showed me how to saddle it and groom it, and I even have my own truck. Tex said I can take it out whenever I want."

"But you don't know how to drive."

"Tex is going to teach me tomorrow. He says I can drive it over the ranch without a license."

"You're kidding!"

"He's being so nice, Tamera. He's going to teach me how to round up and rope cattle, too. It's like he's trying to make all our wishes come true."

"So I guess your mother didn't take one look and decide she hates it, huh?"

"She's floating around with this big smile on her face like she's in heaven."

"And it sounds like you don't hate it too much either."

"Can you imagine, Tamera—my own truck and a CD player in my room."

"Boy, you sure changed your mind in a hurry," Tamera said bitterly. "Who was saying only yesterday that she would never survive without me? Sounds to me like you're surviving without me just fine."

"No, I'm not," Tia said. "I really miss you but—"

"You miss me for five seconds in between driving your very own truck and riding your very own horse. Some traitor you turned out to be. Now you won't want to come home again."

"I didn't say that," Tia said in a hurt voice. "Of course I want to come back, and of course I'm missing you and Detroit. But if I have to be somewhere different, things could be a lot worse."

"Everyone was asking about you at school today," Tamera said. "That guy Philip was asking about you."

"The one who has the locker next to mine?"

"Uh-huh."

"What did he say?"

"He asked where you were and when you were coming back."

"Are you serious, Tamera? I didn't think he'd even noticed I existed."

"So, you see you have to come back now," Tamera

said, trying not to feel too bad for lying about Philip. He still didn't know Tia existed.

"I'm going to school here tomorrow, just to sit in on some classes and see what it's like," Tia said. "I'll call you and tell you all about it. Tex has arranged for someone to pick me up in the morning, so that I don't feel so strange. I'm going to feel strange anyway. I hate walking in on a lot of new people. Do you think I should wear my favorite jeans? I bet girls here don't wear skirts because they ride horses." She paused as she heard her name being called.

"Whoops. Gotta go. Tex has been barbecuing what he calls steaks—they look like half a cow to me. I guess they're ready. Talk to you tomorrow then. Bye."

She put the phone down and ran down the hall. At the other end of the phone line, Tamera put the phone slowly back into its cradle.

"Was that Tia?" Ray asked. "How's she liking it so far?"

"She likes it," Tamera said. "She sounds like she's settling in just great."

"That's good," Ray said.

"No, it isn't. It's terrible. I want her to hate it," Tamera said. "Now it sounds like she never wants to come back."

Chapter 6

The next morning Tia took great care to look just perfect. She put on the jeans with the rips in the knees and a white knitted crop top. She topped off the outfit with a denim hat with a big sunflower on the front.

"Cool," she said to her image in the mirror as she went out of her room. Lisa and Tex were sitting at the table together, drinking coffee.

"Eat some breakfast before you go, honey," Lisa said, getting up from the table. "Do you want me to fix you something?"

"You sit right where you are," Tex commanded, making Lisa sit down again. "I'll have Maria whip her up a batch of pancakes and maybe a ham steak to go with it, or maybe a couple of eggs with some bacon and home fries?"

"No thanks, I couldn't eat a thing," Tia said with a shudder at the thought of bacon and home fries."I'm so nervous."

"Nothing to be nervous about, honey," Lisa said. "You're a nice person. Everyone likes you. You'll get along just fine."

"And the kids are all looking forward to meeting you," Tex said. "I told them all about you. RaeAnn should be along any moment to pick you up."

Maria came out of the kitchen, smiling at Tia. "Don't forget your lunch," she said, holding out an enormous man's lunch box. Tia couldn't say she didn't want it without being rude. She took it and nearly dropped it, it was so heavy.

The other half of that cow must be in here, she thought.

The dogs jumped up, barking, at the sound of a truck. Tia followed Tex outside.

"Hi there, RaeAnn," Tex called. "This is Tia. You take good care of her, you hear?"

A blond girl smiled down at Tia. "Sure thing, Mr. Hunter. Hi there, Tia. Hop on up," she said. Tia took in the blond curls tumbling over her shoulders and the wide blue eyes and decided that RaeAnn looked like a large Barbie doll.

"Hi," she said, feeling suddenly shy as she climbed into the truck.

RaeAnn took off again, tires spraying gravel. "I know y'all are going to like it here, Tia," RaeAnn said. "It's a real friendly school. And everyone likes Tex. I hear he's thinking of marrying your ma. That's so great. Everyone around here has been telling him for years that it was about time he got himself married and settled down."

She turned to Tia and gave her a big smile. "So y'all are from Detroit city? I'm just dying to hear what it's like living in the big city. Aren't y'all scared of all the shootings and violence and gangs?"

Tia laughed. "Right now I live in a very nice suburb. We don't get any shootings or gangs. But even when my mom and I lived in the city, it wasn't as bad as people think. My sister and I ride buses all over the city."

"You have a sister? Is she here, too?"

"No, she stayed back in Detroit with her dad," Tia said. She swallowed hard as she thought of Tamera, so far away.

"Oh, so your parents got divorced?" RaeAnn asked.

"He's not my dad, too," Tia said. "It's just that—"

"But you said she was your sister—you mean half sister?"

Tia decided that RaeAnn wasn't giving her a lot of time to talk. "We're twins, but we were adopted by different families," Tia said. "We only just found each other again. That's why it's so hard to split up now."

"It must be," RaeAnn said, looking at Tia with sympathy. "You poor thing. What a romantic story. They should make a movie out of it. I just love movies, don't you?"

"Yeah, they're great."

"You're so lucky in the big city. I bet you get all the new movies months before they come to us. Not that there's a movie theater closer than Abilene."

"So what do you guys do for fun around here?" Tia asked.

"Not much," RaeAnn said. "The boys go shootin' jackrabbits and stuff, and we have barbecues and dances sometimes in the gym at school or at church, but most of the time it's pretty boring. It livens up during football season. We have a great team—the Buckeye Bulldogs. I made it to the cheerleading squad this year. If you're here in the summer, you can try out. We have so much fun, riding with the team to all the away games. Are you a cheerleader at your school?"

"No," Tia said. She was about to say that she thought cheerleading was a dumb thing to do, but then she shut up. Obviously cheerleading was a big deal to RaeAnn.

"I guess it's harder to make the squad at a big-city school," RaeAnn said kindly. "But you might make it here. You're petite and real cute-looking. I could help you and show you the routines if you like. It's nice to be involved in school activities."

"What else is there to do at your school?" Tia asked. "What activities do they have for girls?"

"Basketball in the winter and softball in the summer," RaeAnn said. "Cheerleading's what we do during football season. Then there's the Future Homemakers Club and the Four H, of course. That's really big around here. Some of us raise calves or poultry . . ."

"Sounds like a blast," Tia said.

RaeAnn didn't pick up the sarcasm. "It sure is," she said, smiling at Tia again. "I know you're going to love it. We're all real friendly." Then her smile faded. "I just wish I'd known ahead of time," she said softly. "I hope you don't mind me mentioning it, but I could have lent you some jeans to wear on your first day."

"What do you mean?" Tia said, confused. "I have jeans."

"Yeah, but . . . I guess y'all were real poor in the city, huh? I couldn't help noticing that your jeans are all old and torn."

Tia didn't know whether to laugh or be angry. "RaeAnn," she said, "these jeans are what kids wear to be fashionable in the city. They cost me fifty dollars."

"Like that? With the rips in them?" RaeAnn asked. She shook her head. "You can get yourself a real nice new pair around here for under twenty dollars. I reckon you got yourself ripped off. Get it—rips? Ripped off? Oh, I'm so funny sometimes." Tia smiled politely.

RaeAnn stopped laughing. "I'm sorry. I didn't mean to hurt your feelings. I guess I've seen girls wearing old ripped-up stuff on MTV and in the magazines, but I thought that was just like a joke, not real life. I mean, jeans like that wouldn't last two minutes with the kind of work we do around here."

Tia had to look down hard so that she didn't grin. She couldn't wait to tell Tamera this! But then she realized that the other kids at school would probably think the same way as RaeAnn, and she didn't want anyone feeling sorry for her. I'd better choose something more normal tomorrow, she thought. Tamera was right. I should have bought some new jeans. I wish you were here with me right now, Tamera, she thought. I have a feeling this isn't going to be too easy. I need someone to share it with me.

"So, do you have a boyfriend at home, Tia?" RaeAnn asked.

"Not at the moment," Tia said. "How about you?"

"I've been dating the same guy since seventh grade," RaeAnn said. "His name's Marley. He's a real hunk—you should see him throw that football!"

They were coming to a small town. On the corner was a general store with a gas pump out in front. Behind it, Tia could see the white spire of a church and then a modern brick school building.

"Here we are," RaeAnn said. "I'm not sure whether you're supposed to be coming to my classes with me all day. I guess I'd better take you into the principal's office. Mr. Hoskins will know what you're supposed to be doing." She leaned over to Tia as she pulled the truck into a parking space. "Don't mind if they stare at your jeans. They won't say anything unkind. They're real friendly, like I said."

Tia climbed down from the truck and walked with RaeAnn across the schoolyard. She was conscious of a lot of stares, and she wished and wished that she hadn't worn the jeans. If they were all as clueless as RaeAnn, they'd feel sorry for her, and she'd hate that.

"This here's Tia. You know, the one who's staying out at Bar T with Tex. Tia, this is Mary Lou, Laurie Beth, Charles Louis, and—"

Tia wondered if there was some law in Buckeye, Texas, that you have to have two first names.

"And Pete," RaeAnn finished. Tia was glad that at least one person apart from her had only one name.

"What was your name again?" one of the girls asked.

"Tia," she said. "Just plain Tia."

"That's a real pretty name, Tia," the girl said with a big too-sweet smile. "I know you're going to love it here."

Tia managed a smile back as she followed RaeAnn up the front steps and into the principal's office.

The principal was a big man with reddish hair and a sweating freckled face. He got up when Tia came in and held out his hand to her. "Welcome, little lady," he said. "I'm Bob Hoskins, the principal of this school. Sit right down and make yourself at home."

Tia tried to imagine Principal Vernon telling any student to make herself at home.

"Tex has told us all about you. I understand you're here to check us out, is that right?"

Tia smiled shyly.

The principal handed her a sheet of paper. "I've drawn up a little schedule of classes I thought would be right for you, seeing that you're a sophomore."

Tia looked at it, blinked, then looked again. "Uh,

excuse me. This is my schedule?" she stammered. "I've got home ec, then consumer math?"

"That's what most of our girls choose to take," the principal said.

Tia took a deep breath. "Mr. Hoskins, I know I'm only here visiting right now, so I suppose it doesn't really matter, but I'm in geometry at home, I'm a straight-A student, and I plan to go into science. I don't ever see myself taking home ec or consumer math."

Mr. Hoskins went on smiling at her as if he found her amusing. "Right now geometry is only offered in the junior year," he said. "And I think you'll find the consumer math very interesting, if you're planning to run a household and balance a budget someday. And I'd try out the home ec, if I were you. Just because you see yourself as a future career woman doesn't mean that you won't need to know how to look after your family someday."

Tia felt as if she might explode any moment, but she managed to hold her breath until she calmed down. She got to her feet. "It's only for a week, I guess. But if you don't mind, I'll skip the math class and do my own math work in the library. I've brought my book with me. I need more practice on triangle proofs."

The principal opened his mouth, then shut it again. "Fine," he said. "That would be just fine."

Tia left the office feeling that she had won a minor battle. She guessed she could survive home ec for a week. Maybe she'd be able to surprise Tamera with a home-baked pie when she got home. And maybe the other classes wouldn't be as bad as she dreaded.

She managed to survive her first home ec class, but she felt really out of place there. All the other girls seemed to know so much that she didn't. They knew how to use all the kitchen tools, and Tia saw them nudge each other when she had to ask for help. She was glad to go on to English. At least she wouldn't look like a dummy anymore.

In English class they were discussing Robert Frost's poetry.

"So what is the poet talking about in this poem?" the teacher asked.

"About a guy picking apples," one of the boys said.

"Is that what you all think this poem is about?" the teacher asked.

There was a long silence. Tia knew what the poem was about but didn't want to stand out as a smart person on the first day. At last a bored voice spoke from the back of the room. "It's about a man thinking about his approaching death."

Everyone turned around to look at the speaker. Tia turned, too. She hadn't noticed him before. He was a lean boy with copper-colored skin and shining black hair.

"What about the apple part?" the first boy asked. "Why is he talking about apples when he's thinking about death? I don't get it."

"It's an image," the boy in the back said. "He's using the image of picking apples for being in the fall of his life."

"I still don't get it," the first boy said. "Why doesn't he say what he means?"

"Miss Johnson, can we read something else? This is too boring," one of the girls complained. "How about a play, then we can all take parts in it."

For a second, Tia caught the eye of the boy in the back, to let him know that she understood. They exchanged a brief grin.

After class she looked for him, but RaeAnn was doing her job of hostess too well. She grabbed Tia and took her over to a lunch table with her friends.

"So how are you liking it so far?" she asked. "I guess you haven't done too much home ec back home." She grinned to her friends. "She didn't know how to use the apple peeler. Miss Bailey had to show her."

"Do apples come ready peeled in the city?" one of the girls asked. Tia hadn't yet managed to sort out Mary Lou from Laurie Beth. The whole table laughed as if this was very funny.

Tia looked around to see if she could see the boy from English class again, but he wasn't in the cafeteria.

"I was telling her too bad she wasn't here for the football season," RaeAnn said. "Life is so exciting then. We have pep rallies and cheerleading practice every day."

"Too bad you weren't here for the rodeo, Tia," Mary Lou—or was it Laurie Beth—said. "I hear y'all like to ride. You could have taken part in the barrel-racing event."

"You have to ride barrels instead of horses?" Tia asked, confused.

The girls all laughed again. "You're such a kidder," RaeAnn said, slapping Tia's arm. "I just love that big-city sense of humor."

Tia decided to shut up after that. She was beginning to feel that she had landed on a strange planet and she didn't speak the same language. She ate the apple and a piece of cheese in her lunch and threw away two steak sandwiches, each about an inch thick.

As she followed the other girls out of the cafeteria, she looked up and saw the boy sitting on a bench, reading a book.

She touched RaeAnn's arm. "Who's he?" she asked.

"You mean Paco?"

"Paco? That's his name?"

"Nickname," RaeAnn said. "His real name is Francisco. He's half Cherokee Indian, half Mexican, and half African American and maybe quarter German . . ."

"That's one and three quarters," Tia said, grinning.

"What are you—some kind of math whiz?" RaeAnn demanded.

"He seems very smart," Tia said.

"Yeah, a real bookworm. And not real friendly either. Keeps himself to himself," RaeAnn said.

Tia wanted to go over to speak to him, but RaeAnn and the others were already sweeping her toward the girls' bathroom to fix their hair.

After lunch RaeAnn went to math class and Tia went to the library. She was in the middle of working through a math proof when she looked up to see the lean, dark-haired boy pass her table. She smiled at him. He came over and pulled out a chair beside her.

"Hi," he said. "I'm Paco—are you new here?"

"I'm Tia. I'm just visiting," Tia said.

"Good," he said, leaning across to look at Tia's math book. "You wouldn't want to be here for long."

"Those kids are pretty dumb in that English class," Tia whispered. "I should have thought anybody could see what that poem meant."

"Me, too," Paco said. He glanced at her math book. "You're lucky to be doing geometry. I wanted to skip a year, but they wouldn't let me. Everyone has to be the same here."

"Why don't you go to school somewhere else?" Tia asked, then realized right away that it was a dumb question.

"My old man works on a ranch," Paco said. "There are no other schools close enough. I'm hoping to get into a good college and then catch up on what I've missed."

Tia nodded with sympathy. "My mom's thinking of moving here," she said. "I don't think I'd get into a good college if I came to school here."

There was an annoyed cough from across the library. They looked up to see the librarian frowning at them. "Is this a work-related conversation?" she asked. "Aren't you young people supposed to be in class right now?"

"I have permission to work here," Tia said.

"And I'm doing research," Paco added. He grinned

at Tia. “I’d better go. She’s not known for her sweet temper. See you later then, okay?”

“Okay,” Tia said. “I’m getting a ride home with RaeAnn—maybe lunch tomorrow?”

Paco smiled. “If RaeAnn will let you escape from her clutches,” he said. “She probably won’t want you to talk to me.”

“Why not?”

“I’m weird. I like reading instead of football.” He gave Tia a friendly wave and sauntered out of the library.

Chapter 7

"I have had the best day, honey," Lisa greeted Tia as she arrived home. "Tex taught me how to drive his big old truck, and he showed me over the whole ranch."

She was dressed head to toe in her new Western gear, including the red-and-white bandanna around her throat.

"Not quite the whole ranch, Lisa honey," Tex said, putting a hand on her shoulder. "That would take a couple of weeks by itself."

"Okay, then, Tex showed me over some of the ranch, and I've seen how he ropes steers and separates out the cows he wants."

"Cattle," Tex corrected. "I already pointed that out to you, remember, honey?"

"Of course. I keep forgetting," Lisa said. "Silly

me." She smiled at Tia. "So, how was your day? Did you have a good time at school?"

"It was okay," Tia said carefully.

"And the kids were friendly like I told you?" Tex asked.

"Sure. Very friendly. Everyone was very nice to me," Tia said.

"That's just fine then," Tex said. He patted Lisa's hand. "See, honey. I told you you were worrying for nothing. She liked it just fine." He looked across to Lisa. "How about we all go out for a little ride before dinner?"

"I have homework to do," Tia said.

"Then it's just you and me, honey," Tex said to Lisa. "Go get your jacket."

"Whatever you say, Tex honey," Lisa cooed. "And after we come back, I'm sending Maria home and I'm going to fix you my special chili for dinner." She gave Tia a warning stare. "And we're going to have a little candlelight dinner, just the two of us," she said to Tex. "I'm sure Tia won't mind trying out that fabulous CD player and TV in her room."

Tia picked up her backpack. "I think I'll go to my room now and get started on my homework," she said. She noticed that Tex had completely forgotten his promise to give her a driving lesson. It was as if she didn't exist when her mother was around. The dogs followed her into her room as she flung down her book bag on the bed. "Hi, sweetie pies," she said, making a big fuss over them. At least the dogs were pleased to see her.

A few minutes later, there was a tap on her door. Lisa came in and closed the door behind her. "I hope you don't mind eating alone tonight. Maria's left you a big salad and a guacamole and chips."

"What's all this about a special chili?" Tia asked coldly. "You've never made chili in your life."

"What do you think was in all that luggage?" Lisa asked. "Cans of gourmet chili."

"That's cheating, Mom," Tia said. "Why are you pretending to be something you're not?"

"I'm trying to be the person Tex wants," Lisa said.

"What if that person is not the real you?"

"He can get to know the real me after we're married," Lisa said. "This is the place of my dreams, Tia."

"And he's the guy of your dreams?"

"He's a nice man, and he thinks I'm special," Lisa said. "That's good enough for me."

Later that evening Tia called Tamera.

"I'm surprised you had time to call," Tamera said. "I'd have thought you'd be driving around in your truck or riding your horse or eating another cow at a barbecue."

"I don't know why I even thought I could have a good time here yesterday," Tia said. "It's the most boring place on earth, and I had to go to school today."

"Were they horrible to you?"

"Oh no, they were very nice. But they expected me to take home ec because I'm a girl."

"Are you serious? Did you tell them to get lost?"

"No, that was after they wanted to put me in consumer math instead of geometry."

"Tia! Did you tell them you were a math whiz?"

"Not exactly, but I said I was going to work alone in the library instead of going to math class and the principal said okay."

"Don't they have any honors classes?"

"There are only a hundred kids in the school, Tamera. There's one class for sophomores, one for juniors, and they're pretty bad. The only thing that matters is football and being a cheerleader."

"So I guess you don't want to stick around after all."

"I can't wait to come home."

"Is your mother tired of being a cowgirl yet?"

"No, that's the problem. She's loving it. She's acting like the helpless female and sweet little housewife, Tamera. You wouldn't recognize her. She flutters her eyelashes at Tex and tells him how strong and clever he is."

"Your mother? The same woman who yells at men for opening the door for her? The same woman who once punched a mugger and broke his nose?"

"Yup, that's her. Only now she can't lift an ashtray without asking Tex to help her. And when Tex tells her to do something, she jumps up and does it right away. He even told her what to wear today!"

"She's just playing at being a Texas housewife," Tamera said. "She'll soon get tired of it."

"What if she doesn't, Tamera?" Tia asked. "I'm

scared that maybe this is the real her, and she's waited until now to find her true self."

"Nah," Tamera said. "Your mom is a tough independent woman. She's never going to let a man tell her what to do."

"She is right now. You should see how he corrects her all the time."

"Then you have to do something, Tia," Tamera said.

"Like what?"

"You have to make her see that she doesn't like it in Texas and she doesn't like being bossed around."

"How?"

"I don't know. You're supposed to be the brainy one. You'll think of something."

"I certainly have enough time," Tia said. "I'm sitting here all alone in my room with two dogs, watching reruns of *The Brady Bunch* on TV while my mother is cooking Tex a cozy candlelight dinner."

"Yuck!" Tamera said. "You'd better go to work fast, girl, or you're stuck in home ec for life."

After she put the phone down, Tia sat staring out into space. She felt sick and scared inside. What if her mom really did decide to stay here and she was stuck in this room forever? She had thought it was so pretty when she first saw it. Now it seemed like a beautiful prison. And RaeAnn and Laurie Beth as her friends, instead of Tamera and her friends back home, and a future of cheerleading and dumb classes?

Tia glared at the *Brady Bunch* kids leaping excitedly

around the screen. "I'm so lucky to have sisters like you," Cindy was saying.

Tia turned off the set. She would never survive here. Tamera was right. She had to do something, and quick!

At lunchtime the next day, Tia made an excuse to get away from RaeAnn and the others in the cafeteria. She found Paco sitting on the same bench in the shade, reading a thick science-fiction book.

"Hi," she said, sitting down beside him.

He looked up and smiled at her. "Are you sure you want to be seen with me?" he asked. "It's going to be bad for your image."

Tia smiled back at him. "I don't think I want my image to be a clone of RaeAnn and her friends. You're the only person I've met since I got here that I can really talk to."

"That's because we're two of a kind and we don't belong here," Paco said.

"What do you mean?" Tia asked.

Paco grinned. "We're smart," he said. "You have to like football and driving trucks and think schoolwork is dumb if you want to fit in here."

"I'm hoping I'm only here on a short visit," Tia said, "but now I'm not so sure. My mom seems to be having a ball."

"She'll probably get tired of it soon enough," Paco said. "When she finds out she has to drive seventy miles to the nearest supermarket . . ."

"Tex has his own plane. He's promised her she can go to Dallas whenever she wants in half an hour."

"Oh, right. I'd forgotten that he was a rich guy. That makes it tough. Of course, I'd like it just fine if you stayed. Tell me, what do you guys do for fun up in Detroit?"

Tia sighed. "There's lots to do at school for starters. I belong to a science club and I compete on a math team."

"A math team? What's that?"

"We're called mathletes, and we have interclass competitions all year, and the best kids compete against other schools."

"Cool. And what do you do in the evenings?"

"There's always something going on. My sister likes to hang out at the mall. We've got one of those movie complexes at our mall—you know, sixteen theaters, all showing different movies."

"Holy cow!"

"And some of us like to go to coffee bars and just sit around and talk. I like that."

Paco's warm brown eyes were smiling into hers. "That sounds great, Tia. I'd like it, too. There's nobody to talk to here and nowhere to hang out either."

"So what do you do?" Tia asked.

"Me, personally, or the other kids?"

"You."

Paco hesitated for a moment, then he said quietly, "There's a couple of places I go to where it's real peaceful, down by the creek. I read sometimes, or I write my poetry."

"You write poems?"

Paco put his finger to his lips. "Shh, don't yell it out. They think I'm weird enough already."

"But, Paco, I think it's great. I've tried to put my feelings down in poems a lot of times, and it's hard for me. I'd love to see some of yours."

"I don't know," Paco said hesitantly. "I've never shown them to anybody. I'll have to think about it."

"Maybe you could show me your place by the creek, too," Tia said. "We could go there and you could read me your poems."

"You won't be around that long," Paco said. He got to his feet. "I should be going," he said, "and so should you. The girls won't forgive you for talking to me."

"I don't care," Tia said. "I like talking to you, Paco. I'd rather talk about poetry than about hairstyles and boyfriends."

He turned back and smiled. "See ya around then, Tia. I'll think about what you said."

Then he was gone. Tia watched the easy way he moved off, with the grace of a wild animal. She thought he was the most interesting person she had ever met. Maybe he'll show me his poems when he knows me better, she thought, and maybe we'll go to his special place by the creek and just sit and talk for hours and . . . Then she stopped herself. She didn't want to stick around here long enough to get to know him better, did she?

Chapter 8

When Tia arrived back at the ranch that afternoon, Lisa was dressed in her riding outfit, looking like something from the front page of a Western-wear catalog.

"Go change your clothes, honey," she said to Tia. "Tex is taking us for a ride. He thinks it's about time you got to know your horse."

"Do I have to?" Tia asked. "I'd only be in the way. I'm sure Tex doesn't really want me around."

"It was Tex's idea. He thinks I've been mollycoddling you for too long and letting you have your own way too much. He told me to have you ready to ride the moment you got in."

"Mom, you know I can hardly ride," Tia said. She was about to add, "And neither can you." Then a brilliant idea struck her. All she had to do was make

Tex see that her mother was a phony. If Tex saw that she was totally clueless on a horse, he might not think she was so special.

"Okay, Mom," she said. "I guess we should go out riding while we're here. It's what people do on ranch vacations, isn't it? I'll go get changed."

She ran into her bedroom and put on her riding clothes. Then she went to join Tex and Lisa at the corral. Jose had already saddled up three horses.

"Here she is," Tex said, beaming at her. "Here's our little horsewoman. Following in Mama's footsteps, huh? Jose will help you up. Show her the right way, Jose."

Jose helped Tia to mount the gentle-looking chestnut called Amber.

Tia watched as Jose attempted to help Lisa into the saddle. Blackbird, the feisty little mare that Tex had picked out for her, danced in circles as she tried to mount.

Just you wait, Tia thought. You're going to find out the truth about the great horsewoman pretty soon.

Tex swung himself easily into the saddle of a magnificent palomino. "Okay, let's go," he called.

They set off down a dusty track, and then Tex opened a gate to let them into an open area where cattle stood silhouetted against the horizon.

"We'll take it easy, first time out," Tex said. "Get the feel of the horse today. We'll just go at a nice, gentle lope."

He urged his horse forward. Tia hadn't done much

more than walk before. She felt the horse start to move quicker, and she gripped the saddle horn tightly. It felt like being on a little boat in a rough sea. She hated to think what a fast gallop would feel like if this was a gentle lope. She glanced across at her mother and noticed, with a satisfied smile, that Lisa was holding on to her saddle horn, too. If I could just make her horse go faster, Tia thought. If I could find a way to make it run away with her, then she'd look like a total idiot.

Immediately she had second thoughts. It was too mean, wasn't it? She couldn't play a mean trick on her mother, even if it was for her own good. And what if she hurt herself? Nah, Tia thought. Tex had told them that Western saddles were made so that it was almost impossible to fall out of them. Lisa would be able to hang on to the saddle horn, and it wasn't as if there were any trees to run into.

Do you want to stay here for the rest of your life? Tia asked herself. Then do it, before it's too late.

Her heart was beating very fast as she edged closer to Lisa's horse. She hadn't a clue how to make a horse run off with somebody, but she could see that Lisa's little mare was easily spooked from the way it danced around whenever she got too close.

Tex was out ahead of them, and Lisa was busy talking to him, telling him a story about her imaginary childhood and how she always used to ride her friend's pony. Tia held her breath and leaned over to Lisa's horse. Then she gave it a gentle slap on the rear.

She never imagined she'd have such instant success. Blackbird shot away in a flat-out gallop. Tia's horse, Amber, pricked up its ears, and before she could do anything to stop it, it surged forward after Blackbird. Tia grabbed at the saddle horn. It was all she could do to prevent herself from being thrown out of the saddle.

"Whoa, what's going on here?" Tex yelled as they passed him.

Tia's horse had its ears back flat against its head now. It was running at full speed, ahead of Lisa's horse. The wind in Tia's face almost took her breath away. Ground flashed past her in a blur. She pulled on the reins with all her strength. She hadn't realized how strong horses were before. Amber ignored her shouts and her tugs at the reins. She came to a bale of hay lying in her path and soared over it in one giant stride. Tia shut her eyes and hung on, feeling herself thrown around in the saddle when Amber landed again. She was really scared now.

"Mama, help me!" she yelled. "Make it stop!"

"Hang on, baby. I'm coming." Lisa's voice came to her over the wind in her ears, as if from very far away. Then gradually Tia saw her mother's horse draw even with hers. Lisa reached out and grabbed Tia's reins. Then she yelled, "Whoa! Stop!" and both horses skidded to a halt.

Tia and her mother sat there, gasping, as Tex caught up with them.

"Thanks, Mom," Tia managed to say. "I couldn't get her to stop."

"That was a very foolish thing to do, young lady!" Tex yelled at Tia. For a moment she wondered if he could possibly know that she had tried to spook Lisa's horse. But he went on, "You think you're a jockey or something? You don't know that horse well enough and you don't know my land well enough to go at that speed yet. You could have done serious damage to my horse, and to yourself, too."

"I'm sorry," Tia said. There was no point trying to explain that she hadn't wanted to go fast at all, she had just wanted Lisa's horse to run away with her.

"If your mama wasn't such a fine little horsewoman, you might be lying in a ditch by now," Tex said, "and my horse might be tangled up in barbed wire." He gazed adoringly at Lisa. "That was a fine piece of riding there, honey. You are some horsewoman."

"You don't think I'd just sit there and let my baby hurt herself, do you?" Lisa said as if she spent most of her time doing daring rescues on horseback.

"You are a lucky girl to have a mama like yours," Tex said.

The moment she got back to her room, Tia called Tamera.

"Help, it's getting worse," she wailed. "I did what you suggested and tried to scare my mom into hating it here. But it didn't work that way." She told Tamera what had happened. "Now she thinks she's the rodeo queen," Tia said. "The problem is that she really did do some fancy riding to save me. Tex keeps telling her how wonderful she is. What am I going to do, Tamera? I really need you! If only you were here with me, I know we'd come up with something together."

"But I can't be with you, Tia," Tamera said. "I'm leaving for Disney World on Saturday, remember?"

"I know," Tia said. "I just wish . . ."

"What?"

"Nothing," Tia said. "Have a great time at Disney World."

After Tia hung up, Tamera stood there for a long time, holding the phone in her hand.

"What the matter, princess?" Ray asked, putting a hand on her shoulder and making her jump. "You look like you're a million miles away. Missing your sister, I suppose?"

"Dad," Tamera said slowly, "I've been thinking. I'm just not sure how much fun Disney World will be with just the two of us. I mean, you won't want to go on any of the scary rides, will you?"

"I don't know—" Ray began, but Tamera went right on. "And I won't want to go on those rides by myself."

"So, are you saying you don't want to go?" Ray asked.

"I'm saying it won't be the same without Tia there to share it with me. And I wouldn't want you to spend all that money and then find out that I wasn't having the greatest time in the world."

"That's very thoughtful of you, Tamera," Ray said.

"But I know how long you've wanted to go to Disney World. It could be fun with just the two of us."

"Dad, we'd go on It's a Small World and we wouldn't be able to get that song out of our heads, and it would drive us crazy," Tamera said. "And the lines would probably be too long over spring break. We'd never get to go on the Indiana Jones ride. So I was wondering . . ."

"Yes, Tamera?"

"I was wondering if there was any way I could cash in my plane ticket or get it rewritten to Dallas so that I could be with Tia."

"Tamera, you know that's impossible," Ray said. "Tex invited Lisa and Tia so that they could see whether ranch life was right for them. Tia would never be able to decide if you were there, too. And they wouldn't want you there, either." His arm tightened around her shoulder in a hug. "You've got to let Tia give this a chance, honey."

"She's given it a chance, Dad, and she totally hates it already," Tamera said.

Ray chuckled. "She's only been there a few days. How can she possibly know already?"

"They tried to make her take home ec at school, and they wouldn't give her the math class she wants, and she feels like a total outsider, Dad. That's why I want to go down there—because Tia needs my help to make her mother see that Texas is all wrong for her."

"I take it Lisa doesn't hate it as much as Tia does?"

"She pretends that she loves it. She's letting that

Tex guy boss her around, and she's even wearing an apron. We have to get her out of there before it's too late."

"I don't think it's right for you to interfere, Tamera. It's Lisa's life, after all. She has a right to choose her own happiness, and if she's happy there, then you have to accept that."

"But she can't really be happy there, Dad," Tamera said. "You know that Lisa is a city person as well as I do. And she'll be bored to tears—there's nothing for her to do all day." She turned to her father and wrapped her arms around his neck. "Please, Daddy. Let me do this. I can't let Tia down."

"I don't know. . . ." Ray began.

Tamera gazed, pleading, into his eyes. "Please, Daddy? Do it for me?"

"Okay," Ray said. "I tell you what—if Lisa and Tex say that it's okay for you to be there, then you can have your ticket. But if Lisa goes on thinking that she loves it down there and she loves Tex, too, then I'm afraid you girls have both got to accept the fact that Tia's not going to live here anymore."

"You're the best father in the world," Tamera said. "Thank you, thank you, thank you. If we can save Tia and bring her back here, I'll be grateful forever."

"Does that mean you'll wash your dirty dishes? And not drop your scarf in the front hall?"

"I didn't say I was going to be perfect," Tamera said as she ran up to her room to call Tia.

"Hi, it's me," she said when Tia picked up the phone. "Are you alone?"

"When am I ever not alone?" Tia said. "My mom and Tex are sitting out on the porch, watching the stars. Not that there's anything else to watch out here. What's up? You just spoke to me ten minutes ago."

"I've been talking things over with my dad," Tamera said. "I decided that Disney World would be no fun without you. So I asked my dad if I could have the money for a ticket to Dallas instead."

"You're going to come here?" Tia shrieked. "Tamera, that's incredible. Why would you do that?"

"Because I have to help get you out of there before it's too late," Tamera said.

"That is so nice of you to give up your chance to go to Disney World for me." Tia sounded close to tears.

"There's one condition," Tamera said. "My dad said that Lisa and Tex have to give their permission first."

"I'll find a good moment and ask my mother," Tia said. "It probably won't be until the morning. I don't want to go out there and find my mother kissing him. Call you back tomorrow, okay?"

"Okay. Good luck," Tamera said. "Twin power to the rescue, huh?"

"I hope," Tia said. "I don't know how much more of this I can take."

Chapter 9

The next morning Tia waited until she saw Tex's truck disappearing in a cloud of dust, then she went to find her mother sipping coffee in the kitchen.

"Hey, Mom, guess what," she said. "Tamera's trip to Disney World got canceled."

Lisa looked up from her coffee. "Oh no, that's too bad. What happened?"

"It seems that they booked the wrong dates or something. I talked to her last night and she's so upset—you know how she was looking forward to it."

"Poor Tamera," Lisa said. "I hope the trip can be rescheduled for her."

"It wouldn't be at least until summer," Tia said. "So she's all alone for spring break with nothing to do." Her voice dropped to scarcely more than a whisper. "So I wondered if she could maybe come here and join us? Ray said he'd pay for the ticket."

"Tamera wants to come here? Oh no. No way."

"Mom, please. I'm missing her so much, and it's a big house, and there's plenty of room for her with me. We wouldn't disturb you and Tex."

Lisa shook her head firmly. "I'm sorry, Tia, but there's no way you're inviting Tamera here. Tex wanted us to get to know each other better—away from your sister."

"Oh yeah, right," Tia said. "He doesn't really want me here. He yelled at me on that ride yesterday."

"You were stupid to go galloping off like that. He was worried for you."

"He was worried for his horse. I was an afterthought. And he promised to take me out driving, but he seems to have forgotten about it. If Tamera came, we could give you and Tex more time to be together."

"No, Tia. Tex wouldn't want her here, I'm sure. In spite of what you say, he wants to get to know you better. He wants you to like it here. I'm sure you two would get along just fine if you tried."

"So you're saying there's no point in asking Tex?"

"I'm not going to ask him," Lisa said, "and neither are you."

"You're not being fair to me, Mom," Tia said.

"No, Tia. You're not being fair to me," Lisa said. "It would be nice if you were happy because I'm happy for once."

"You're not really happy," Tia said. "You're playing at being somebody you're not. It can't last, you know. Tex is bound to find out in the end that you're not this person you have created."

Then she strode out of the kitchen, not listening to what Lisa was yelling after her. She ran back to her room, and with trembling fingers, she dialed Tamera's number.

"I have to whisper, because I can't risk having my mother hear me," she said.

"Did you ask her? What did she say?"

"She said no way."

"Oh, that's too bad," Tamera said with a nervous giggle.

"Why?"

"Because I already booked my flight."

"Tamera, you didn't!"

"I figured you needed help, whatever anyone else said. How about if I tell my dad that it's just fine and come anyway? Your mom wouldn't send me back once I was there, would she?"

"That wouldn't work," Tia said. "You'd need someone to meet you at the airport."

"So I'll get a taxi."

"Tamera, get serious. This place is out in the boonies, and I mean the boonies. It took over two hours by car."

Tamera sighed. "I guess that's that, then. And now my dad's canceled Disney World because I told him I didn't want to go. Now we'll both have miserable vacations."

"I wish you could come, Tamera," Tia said. "But I just don't see how."

"I'm not going to let you go without a fight, Tia," Tamera said. "You're supposed to be the smart one. Come up with a way to get me out to you."

As Tia got ready for school, she wished that she had made Tex give her those driving lessons he'd promised. Then she could have taken the truck and picked up Tamera herself.

Get real, she told herself. You might learn to drive around a ranch in a truck, but there's no way you're ready for a freeway and Dallas Airport—and you don't have a license to drive on real roads anyway.

Her brain was still working overtime as she got into RaeAnn's truck and headed for school. A couple of times she glanced at RaeAnn, wondering if she could ask her for help. RaeAnn had thought that her life story was romantic. Maybe she'd want to help get her and Tamera back together. But she was also an airhead, Tia decided. She'd probably blab all over the school and Tex would get to hear about it, and Tia would be in big trouble. RaeAnn probably would, too. This was a small community, and Tex was a bigshot.

I'll just have to survive the rest of the time here alone, Tia thought. And then it hit her. What if she had to survive two whole years of school here, with home ec and football and RaeAnn and her friends? Tia shook her head firmly. There was no way her mother could do that to her, was there? Lisa knew she was smart. She wanted her to go to the best college. She wouldn't spoil her chances by sending her to a terrible school. If only Tex and Lisa would let her live with Tamera during the school year . . . but she couldn't see Lisa wanting to give up her baby either.

"Doomed," Tia muttered to herself.

"What?" RaeAnn asked.

"Nothing," Tia said. "Just thinking of some song lyrics."

"Oh, do you like music? I just love it. Maybe you'd like to come over to my place sometime and we'll play some CDs. I've got every country-and-western song ever recorded, but I still like 'Achy Breaky Heart' best, don't you? Even though it's an oldie."

Tia gazed at her reflection in the truck window. "Doomed," she mouthed to herself.

The day went by painfully slowly. Then in English class, she opened her book and a piece of paper fluttered out. She grabbed it and found herself looking at a poem, written in bold, black slanting script:

> Sit, a stone, and survey
> Until love and life pass away,
> Rest, a rock on the shore,
> Until fate and death are no more,
> Then, as a new moon, alone,
> Arise and face the unknown.

It was unsigned, but Tia knew right away who had written it. Paco must have slipped it into the book when she left her book bag on the bench during home ec. She turned around to him, but he was busy writing and didn't look up. Tia had to wait impatiently until lunchtime, when she shook off RaeAnn and waited for him.

"Paco, it was beautiful," she said. "Thank you so much for sharing it with me."

He looked at her shyly. "You really think it was okay?"

"Okay? It was great," Tia said. "You have a real gift for words. Lots of images in it, too." She shared a knowing smile with him.

"I've never shown my poetry to anyone before," he said.

"I'd love to see more things you've written," Tia said.

Paco shook his head. "I copy it all into a big old notebook at home," he said. "I don't want to risk bringing that to school. The kids would have a field day if they found it. They'd tease me forever."

"They should be proud there's someone like you at their school," Tia said.

"Right," he said bitterly. "I don't throw a football well. I don't run fast. I don't drive a fancy new truck. That's all that matters here." He paused, drawing circles in the dust with his sneaker toe. "If you like," he said, "maybe we could go to my place after school and pick up the book. Then we could take it down to the creek and I'll read you some of the poems."

"I'd like that, Paco," Tia said. "But RaeAnn gives me a ride home."

"I could run you home afterward," Paco said. "If you'd like."

Tia smiled. "Okay," she said. "I'll tell RaeAnn."

RaeAnn's eyes shot wide open, making her look even more like a Barbie doll, when Tia told her. "Y'all are riding home with Paco? What for?"

"We want to discuss something he's doing for English class," Tia said, deciding that it might be simpler to make it sound like an assignment and not a date.

RaeAnn wrinkled her nose. "Rather you than me," she said. "Okay, see y'all in the morning then?"

Tia nodded. "Thanks, RaeAnn," she said.

After school she found Paco by a rusty beat-up truck. It looked so old that Tia couldn't imagine how it could still run, especially over the bumpy roads around Buckeye.

"Great wheels, huh?" Paco asked, as if he could tell what she was thinking. "It's held together by string, wire, and prayers. But it gets me around. You're lost out here without transportation."

The truck belched smoke and rattled alarmingly as they left the parking lot. A group of older boys looked up as they passed and called out something rude, which Tia couldn't hear over the noise of the truck. Paco acted as if he hadn't heard either.

They turned off the paved road soon after they left town and bumped along a dusty track until they came to a ramshackle house with chickens scratching in the front yard and washing flapping on a line.

Paco got out. "Wait here," he said. "I'll go get my book. I'd rather not ask you inside."

"Okay, I'll wait," Tia said. She could hear loud music and the sound of a baby crying as he opened the front door. She imagined him trying to do homework, or write his poetry, with all that noise going on. No wonder he tried to escape, she thought, and felt very sorry for him. All her life her mother had given her everything she needed to study and been so proud of her when she did well in school. And she had taken all that for granted. She wished there was something she could do to help Paco, but she couldn't think what.

Paco came running out again after a few seconds, a big book tucked under his arm and two cans of soda in his hand.

"Here," he said. "I thought you might be thirsty. There weren't any snacks left, or I'd have brought something to eat, too."

Again Tia felt guilty when she remembered throwing away half her lunch. Maybe Paco didn't get enough to eat. Maybe he would have wanted her extra sandwiches.

"It's okay," she said. "I'm hardly ever hungry. I throw away half my lunch every day. They give me way too much."

"I'm always hungry," Paco said. "I guess I'm just a growing boy, huh?"

"You can have some of mine tomorrow if you want," Tia said.

The truck bumped and lurched along a narrow

track between barbed-wire fences. Then it dipped between sandy banks and came out, at last, beside a little stream. There were shady cottonwood trees growing along the creek, and wildflowers dotted the grassy banks.

"Paco, this is beautiful," Tia said, jumping down onto the sand.

"It's always peaceful here," he said. "Most of the kids go a couple of miles downstream, where there's a swimming hole."

Tia opened the soda he offered her and walked out onto the sandy beach beside the stream. "It's like a different world," she said.

Paco nodded. "When I was little, I used to come here and pretend it was my magic kingdom. I was the king, of course. That big rock used to be my throne."

Tia looked at him with understanding. "I used to pretend all the time when I was little, too," she said. She went over to the big rock. "Am I allowed to sit on it, or is it just for the king?"

"You can sit on it," he said. "You're visiting royalty."

Tia smiled and sat down. The rock felt warm and smooth. Paco joined her. "Can I look?" she asked, pointing to the book in his hands. "Or do you want to read to me?"

He handed her the book. "You can look," he said. "I feel kind of weird reading my stuff out loud."

She opened the book.

"I was pretty young when I started," Paco said. "The first poems are bad."

Tia's eyes skimmed down the page.

> Color is a lovely thing
> To help our sight.
> Blue for sky, green for grass,
> Brown for the road on which we pass,
> And black for night.

The writing was a child's first printing. "How old were you when you wrote this one?"

Paco shrugged. "First grade. I'd just learned to write."

"Paco, you were a child genius." She flicked on through the pages. "I wish I had your talent," she said at last. "If I were you, I'd make a portfolio of the best of these and send it in with your college application. I'm sure someone will give you a scholarship."

Paco's eyes lit up. Tia noticed how they really sparkled. "You think so?" he asked. "You think someone would give me a scholarship?"

"I bet they would. You're good, Paco. You have to believe in yourself."

"It's not easy," he said. "Nobody else believes in me."

"The teachers must know that you're smart."

"The teachers think I'm a pest, because I'm always asking questions and arguing with what they say. They like kids who sit there and don't say anything."

"All of them? The English teacher seemed to think you were pretty smart."

"Maybe, but she's the only one and she doesn't like me talking too much, or the rest of the class gets antsy." He looked at Tia. "Don't let them send you to school here," he said. "You have to make your mother see that it would wreck your chances. This place kills good brains."

"You've survived all this time."

"I've had to," he said. "I have no choice." He picked up a small rock and skimmed it across the smooth surface of the water. "Nobody in my family ever went to college," he said. "They think I'm crazy because I want to finish high school."

"Don't listen to them," Tia said. "Don't let anyone stomp on your dreams, Paco."

"I'll try not to," he said. "Now you're here, anything seems possible."

He was looking at her so intensely that she began to feel uncomfortable. "I should be getting back, I guess," she said. "I didn't tell anyone where I was going."

"They'll know," Paco said with a grin. "You wouldn't believe the grapevine here. Everyone knows everything right away."

He got to his feet and held out his hand to help Tia up. Tia was aware of his hand, warm and firm, holding hers.

"Come on," he said. "I'll drive you home."

As they sat side by side in the truck, Tia wrestled with the question she wanted to ask him. He was so happy to have her there that it seemed mean to ask his help to get her out, but she couldn't think of anyone else she could ask.

"Paco," she began hesitantly, "I've got a favor to ask you."

"Okay, go ahead."

"I wondered if you could possibly drive to the airport one day and pick up my sister."

Paco looked astonished. "Y'all have a whole bunch of fancy trucks sitting there at the ranch."

"I know, but I can't ask anyone there to go pick up my sister because nobody knows she's coming but me."

"It's a surprise?"

"I'll say," Tia said. She smiled at him shyly. "Okay, this is what's happening. Tamera and I are twins."

"And you're missing her?"

"More than that. I need her help to work on my mother. She's acting like she loves it here, Paco. If I can't make her hate it before she says okay and marries Tex, then I'm stuck here forever. When Tamera and I are together, we come up with the greatest ideas."

"So she's coming to help you make your mother hate it here?" He grinned. "I can see why you haven't told anyone she's coming."

"It's worse than that," Tia said. "My mom actually said there was no way that Tamera could come."

"So you could get in big trouble?"

"I guess, but it's worth it if we can make my mother open her eyes."

He looked at her steadily. "You're asking a lot of me," he said.

"You don't think the truck will make it that far? I'd pay for gas," Tia said.

Paco shook his head. "The truck will make it just fine. I meant helping you get away from here, just when I've found the first person I could ever talk to."

"I'm sorry, Paco," Tia said. "That was selfish of me—and you'd be the only reason I'd want to stay. But you said yourself that I should get away while I could."

"I know," he agreed. "It's okay. I'll do it. Just tell me when you want me to pick her up."

"Thanks, Paco." Tia went to hug him, then stopped herself at the last second.

"And you'll have to tell me what she looks like, because there's not room for both of you in the truck."

Tia laughed. "She looks like me, Paco. You'll think you're looking at another me."

They drove under the ranch gateway and pulled up outside. The dogs came running out, wagging their tails and jumping up at the truck.

"Somebody likes you here," Paco said.

"Yeah, they're my only friends, except for you," Tia said. She put a hand gently on his arm. "Thanks a million, Paco. You're a real friend. I'm so glad I met you."

"Me, too," he said. "Tell me when you've made your plans, okay?"

"I will. I'll call my sister tonight. And thanks for

sharing your poetry with me, and your magic kingdom."

He nodded. "I'm glad I showed you now. It won't be the same when your sister gets here."

Tia made a face. "I'll probably be locked in my room in disgrace when they find out. But it will be worth it if we can come up with a way to get my mother back to Detroit."

She jumped down from the truck. "Bye, Paco. See you in the morning."

"Bye, Tia," he called as she ran into the house.

Chapter 10

Tia was so busy petting the dogs as she came in that she didn't notice the two people standing in the cool darkness of the living room, waiting for her.

"Where have you been, young lady?" Tex asked, making her jump at the sound of his voice.

"Excuse me?" Tia stopped, just inside the front door.

"I asked you where you've been," Tex said evenly. "Your mother was worried sick when RaeAnn's truck drove past and you weren't in it."

Tia glanced at her watch. "It's only five o'clock," she said. "And nothing is likely to happen to me out here, except maybe getting mugged by a cow."

"I didn't know where you'd got to, baby," Lisa said. "We called RaeAnn's house, and she said you'd gone off with a boy."

"Mom, this guy in my English class and I went to study some poetry together. No big deal. What's with you? You don't freak out at home when I'm a few minutes late."

"You don't know your way around here yet," Tex said. "Your mother was frightened you'd get lost. And you don't know which boys can be trusted."

Tia could feel the angry flush rising. "My mother trusts me at home. She knows I'm not stupid."

"Don't use that tone of voice with me, young lady," Tex said. "That was Paco Juarez's truck, wasn't it?"

"That's right."

"I don't want you seeing him," Tex said. "That family is bad news."

Tia glared at him. "Paco is a nice guy," she said. "He's very smart, and I like talking to him."

"I've just said I don't want you seeing him," Tex repeated, "and I expect you to obey my wishes."

"You're not my father!" Tia yelled. "You can't tell me what to do!"

"Tia!" Lisa exclaimed in horror.

"Well, it's true," Tia said. "He can't boss me around. I'm going to talk to whom I like."

"See, Lisa, I told you you had spoiled her," Tex said. "I told you she'd start running wild if you didn't keep the reins tight."

"I'm not one of your precious horses," Tia snapped. "And my mother didn't spoil me. She brought me up just fine until you came along. I thought she trusted me until now."

"Tia, baby . . ." Lisa went to take a step forward, but Tex put out a hand to restrain her.

"Let me handle this, Lisa," Tex said.

"I'm going to my room," Tia said. She hurried down the hallway before Tex had a chance to say anything more.

She shut the bedroom door behind her and leaned against it, feeling the cool firmness on her warm skin. She hardly ever fought with her mother at home. She hated fights, and she hated Tex.

He's not going to boss me around, she said to herself. She wished Tamera was here right now. She felt as if she was about to cry, and she needed a big hug from her sister. "You have to get me out of here, Tamera," she whispered.

On Saturday morning Paco drove to Dallas airport to meet Tamera's flight. Tia stayed behind at the ranch. She had hardly spoken to Tex since the fight on Thursday. Looking back, she was glad that it had happened. At least she knew, without a doubt now, that she could never be happy living with Tex. Now that she hated him, she didn't feel so bad about deceiving him. She still felt bad about tricking her mom, though.

But I'm doing it for her, she reminded herself. One day she'll thank me for it.

After breakfast on Saturday, Tex nearly blew everything by offering to take them into Dallas to go shopping.

"What a great idea," Lisa said. "I'm suffering from

shopping-withdrawal symptoms, aren't you, Tia honey?"

"You two go," Tia said. "I'd rather stay here."

"But you love shopping, and I hear that Dallas has the best stores—Neiman Marcus, Tia—doesn't that sound good?"

"I don't feel like shopping," Tia said.

"Then we won't go," Tex said. "What do you want to do, Tia?"

It was clear that he was trying to be nice to her. Maybe he realized he had upset Lisa by being so hard on her daughter.

"You two go to Dallas," Tia said. "I'll be fine alone." If they were safely out of the way, then Paco could drive up to the house. If not, then she had to find a way to get Tamera from the gate unnoticed, and that wasn't going to be so easy.

"Oh no," Tex said. "We're not risking you meeting with that boy while we're away."

"Okay, then, you promised to teach me to drive," Tia said. "If you give me a lesson, then I could practice driving around the ranch."

"All right," Tex said. "Let's do it. If you learn how to drive, you won't need to accept rides from that no-good boy."

Tia swallowed back what she wanted to say. Right now she needed Tex's help. She tried to be sweet and obedient as she followed Tex out to the truck. She just prayed that she'd learn quickly enough for Tex to let her take the truck out alone. It would be perfect if she could pick up Tamera at the gate. She was glad that Ray had given her a couple of driving lessons in an empty parking lot once. At least she wouldn't look totally clueless. But the truck seemed huge, and it had gears, too!

Tex showed her how to use the clutch. It took a while for her to get the truck in gear, but once she started moving forward, she found it wasn't too bad after all.

"You're getting the hang of this very quickly, Tia," Tex said. "You'll be driving around on your own in no time at all."

"Do you think I can drive well enough to practice for a while on my own when we're done?" Tia asked as they headed back to the house after driving around for a while. "I feel kind of nervous when you're here, watching me."

"You don't have to be nervous with me," Tex said. "I'm sure we're going to get along just fine together. But you can practice driving on your own, as long as you stay close to the ranch house and don't go off the property."

"Thank you," Tia said, trying to give him her warmest smile. She glanced at her watch. "I think I'll get a snack first."

"See, I knew it," Tex said, looking pleased with himself. "I knew the good fresh air would give you an appetite. We'll have a big barbecue tonight. Maybe we'll invite some folks over to meet y'all."

"It's okay with me if you and my mom go shopping," Tia said. "I really don't mind. I'll just practice driving the truck around."

"I don't think your mother wants to leave you here alone," Tex said.

Okay, so this wasn't going to be so easy, Tia thought. She ate her snack and watched the seconds tick by painfully slowly. Tamera's plane was getting in at ten. That meant she couldn't possibly arrive at the ranch before close to one o'clock.

Tia took milk and cookies back to her room and made sure that she was close to the phone. Now that Tamera was actually coming, Tia felt sick and scared. Her mother was going to be so angry with her, and she had already seen how Tex had yelled at her for riding home with Paco.

Quit worrying, she told herself. What's the very worst they can do to me? Send Tamera back home and make me stay in my room. It's only for a week. I can handle it. And it might just work.

She jumped when the phone rang and snatched up the receiver. It was somebody calling Tex about the barbecue. She waited, watching the phone and willing it to ring.

Just after twelve-thirty, it rang again. Tia grabbed it.

"Hi, Tia?" Paco asked cautiously. "I've picked up the cargo you wanted."

"Where are you?"

"At the gas station in town. Can you get the truck?"

"Sure. I'll meet you at the ranch gate in about fifteen minutes."

She ran out of her room. "Is it okay if I go practice driving now?" she asked.

Tex looked up from his newspaper. "Sure. That's just fine. Remember what I told you—take it easy and don't get yourself in soft sand or you'll spin the wheels and get stuck. Just concentrate on nice smooth forward motion, got it?"

"Yeah, got it. Thanks, Tex," Tia said breathlessly.

"You want me to come with you, baby?" Lisa asked. "I could give you moral support."

"No thanks," Tia said, too quickly. Then she checked herself. "I have to get the confidence to drive alone, thanks, Mom."

She grabbed the keys and ran out to the truck. Whew, that was close! Her hand was shaking so much that she could hardly put the key into the ignition. "You can do this," Tia told herself.

She turned the key, and the engine sprang to life. It sounded more powerful than she had remembered when Tex was with her. She put it into gear and it stalled.

"Foot on the clutch, dummy!" she yelled to herself. She had to do it. Tamera would be waiting for her. This time she let the clutch up very slowly. The truck jerked and started to crawl forward.

"I'm driving!" Tia yelled excitedly.

She gripped the steering wheel with both hands and came around the ranch house. Lisa came to the window to watch her. Tia would have liked to wave, but she was too scared to let go of the steering wheel. She could hear the engine roaring and knew that she should change to second gear, but she was too scared to try it. So she continued at about five miles an hour, down the track toward the front gate.

She stopped a little way from the gate. When she got down from the cab, she found that her knees were shaking so much she could hardly walk. Now she just had to pray that Tex and Lisa hadn't decided to follow her or that one of the ranch hands wasn't around when she met Tamera.

She left the truck and ran down to the gate. After a few minutes, she heard the unmistakable sound of Paco's truck. Then it came into sight, followed by a plume of dust. Paco brought it to a stop right beside Tia. "Hi," he said, smiling down at her. "You were right. She does look just like you."

"Hi, Tia!" Tamera yelled over the truck engine. "Paco has been so nice to me. He's been telling me all about Texas and Tex and the ranch. I feel like I know it already." She jumped down and flung herself into Tia's arms.

"I can't believe you're here," Tia said.

"Me, neither. Isn't this crazy? It's the craziest thing we've ever done."

"I know. I don't know how we're going to hide you or what we're going to do now you're here, but I'm so happy to see you!" Tia danced around, still hugging her sister.

"I'd better get going," Paco called down to them. "You know that Tex doesn't like you talking to me."

"Thanks for everything, Paco. You are the sweetest guy in the world," Tia said, taking Tamera's bag out of the truck, then slamming the door closed. "I'll call you, okay? Maybe we can do something together when Tamera and I get ourselves sorted out."

He gave an embarrassed grin, then drove off.

"He is so nice," Tia said to Tamera.

"I can see that," Tamera said. "And he definitely likes you a lot. He did nothing but talk about you all the way here."

"I like him, too," Tia said.

"So, why do you need me to help you get out of here?" Tamera teased.

"Wait until you see my mother and Tex, then you'll know," Tia said. She walked up to the truck and threw Tamera's bag inside. "Hurry up and get in, in case anyone sees you."

"Who's driving?" Tamera asked cautiously.

"Me."

"Are you serious? You can drive a truck?"

"Sure. I learned this morning."

"Oh, great. That gives me confidence," Tamera teased.

"It's not far and I take it slow," Tia said. "I've only really got the hang of first gear. Okay, duck down so that nobody sees you."

She started the truck on the first try and they set off, bumping at a snail's pace back toward the house.

"Are Tex and Lisa home?"

"Uh-huh. I tried to get them to go out, but they wouldn't go. They're planning a big barbecue for tonight."

"So I'm going to arrive in full view of everybody,"

Tamera said. "And how do you plan to get me inside?"

"Simple—I hope," Tia answered. "I'll park the truck away from the house, then I'll go to my room and open the window for you to come in. Wait until nobody's watching, then come."

"How will I know which window is yours?"

"It'll be the one that's open, and I'll wave."

"Sounds easy enough," Tamera said doubtfully.

"Keep quiet now, we're coming to the house," Tia instructed. Tamera scrunched down on the floor.

"What do we do with my bag?" she asked.

"Leave it in the truck until later. Nobody drives it except me," Tia said. "Now, don't say another word. We're here."

Nobody appeared as Tia parked the truck. "Here goes nothing," she whispered to Tamera. She climbed down and sauntered toward the front door.

"Hi, everyone, I'm back," she called.

Lisa and Tex appeared from the kitchen. "That was quick," Lisa said. "You just left."

"That was enough for the first day," Tia said. "I only just learned, remember."

"You did just fine. I watched you go," Tex said encouragingly.

"You were great, baby. I'm so proud of you," Lisa added. "Come and have lunch. It's all ready. And then we have to get busy preparing for tonight."

"Tonight?" Tia's mind was blank for a second.

"The barbecue. Tex has invited a whole bunch of people to meet us."

"Oh yeah, the barbecue," Tia said.

"We'll need your help to get things ready. Sit down and eat," Tex said.

"Okay," Tia said. "I just need to go to my room first."

She sprinted down the hall, closed her door behind her, and then ran across to the window. It opened easily enough, but there was a screen on the outside. She hadn't noticed it before.

To her horror, she watched Tamera get out of the truck and hurry across the yard.

"Hi, it's me. Let me in," she whispered.

"I can't. I can't move the screen."

"Oh, great. What do we do now?" Tamera sounded close to panic.

"Wait, let me think."

"We don't have time to think," Tamera hissed. "I'm standing out here where anyone can see me. Help me get the screen off this stupid window! You push and I'll pull."

Suddenly the dogs came flying around the corner.

"Tia, there are two big dogs heading for me! What do I do now?" Tamera wailed.

"Don't worry, they're friendly," Tia started to say when the dogs hurled themselves at Tamera, barking and growling.

"Nice doggies," Tamera said weakly, backing against the window. "I thought you said they were friendly! What do I do now, Tia? I didn't come here to be eaten."

The noise brought Tex running. "What's going

on?" he asked, looking curiously at Tamera. "What are you doing, Tia?"

"Nothing. I just went back to the truck to get something and the dogs started barking at me," Tamera said, hoping he wouldn't remember that she and Tia were wearing different color T-shirts.

"That's weird," Tex said. "Quiet, dogs. What's the matter with you?" The dogs stopped barking, but they were still alert and growling under their breath.

"Maybe they're just being good watchdogs," Tamera suggested.

"They don't bark at people they know," Tex said. "They usually like you."

Tamera smiled weakly. "Who knows what goes on in doggy minds. Oh well, I guess I'll just come inside and go to my room."

She and Tia were both holding their breath as Tamera walked into the house beside Tex.

"What was all that about?" Lisa asked, only half looking up.

"No idea," Tex said. "The dogs started growling at Tia. It was the strangest thing. Usually they can't wait to play with her."

"Maybe I smell funny today," Tamera said, and fled down the hall before Lisa could focus on her. Tia opened a door at the end of the hallway and Tamera slid gracefully inside.

"That was awful," she said. "I thought I was going to be eaten alive."

"I guess dogs are smarter than people," Tia commented. "They knew you were a stranger. Tex didn't notice you weren't me. You'd better not leave this room again until the dogs have a chance to meet you. I have to go have lunch now."

"I'm starving," Tamera said. "All I've had is an airline breakfast."

"I'll bring you some food when I can," Tia said. "Just stay put and hide in my closet if anyone comes."

"I feel like a criminal," Tamera said. "I get the feeling I might have done something really stupid coming here."

Tia smiled weakly. "I'm really glad you're here," she said. "I missed you."

"But what am I going to do, now that I'm here? Tell me that. I can't stay hidden in your closet for a week."

"We'll find the right moment to let them know you're here. But not today. They're planning a big barbecue for tonight, so that we can meet people."

"Tia! Come and eat!" Tex's voice echoed through the closed door.

"I have to go," Tia said. "I'm sure it will all work out."

"Oh, sure," Tamera said. "That's what they said on the *Titanic* when they noticed the iceberg."

Chapter 11

Tamera was alone in Tia's room for most of the afternoon. She waited for Tia to bring her something to eat, but Tia didn't appear again. The minutes dragged by. Tamera lay on Tia's bed, tense and ready to hide at the sound of footsteps, wondering what had made her think that coming here was a good idea. What on earth could she do to help Tia? When Lisa and Tex found out, they'd both be in trouble. If Lisa decided to marry Tex, maybe he'd think that Tamera was the troublemaker and forbid Tia to see her again.

Tamera's stomach growled. She went to the door and opened it a few inches. Everything was quiet. She was so hungry now that she was feeling desperate. She wondered if she could get as far as the kitchen without being discovered or torn to pieces by dogs.

Suddenly she heard footsteps on the stone floor. She leaped back inside the room and was halfway into the closet when the door opened.

"You'd make a terrible burglar," Tia said as she closed the door behind her.

"I was getting desperate. I was almost tempted to come out and raid the kitchen. Hunger does that to a person."

"I've brought you some cheese and an apple," Tia said. "It was all I could grab with my mother watching me. Sorry it took so long, but they made me help them get everything ready for tonight."

"I suppose I'm stuck in here tonight while you're at the barbecue," Tamera said gloomily.

"I think it would be smart to stay hidden right now. Tex and my mom are both tense about the barbecue. Not a good moment to bring you out."

"Okay, but don't forget to bring me some food," Tamera said.

Tia disappeared into the shower and changed into jeans and a new Western shirt. "Don't laugh," she said to Tamera. "I've been told to wear it. Now Tex is even telling *me* what to wear."

"Tex told you you had to wear the shirt?"

"You better believe it. And he tells my mom what to wear all the time."

"You really do need my help," Tamera said.

Tia finished getting ready and went out again. Tamera heard the sound of people arriving, loud voices, and laughter. More and more people arrived. It began to get dark. She wondered if she dare turn a light on, then decided that at least she could watch TV.

She was in the middle of one of her favorite comedy shows when a loud voice made her jump. "Tia? What are you doing in there?" Tex was glaring at her through the window. "Get out here right now. You're a hostess here, remember."

Tamera had no choice. If she didn't come out, Tex would come and get her. He might even bring Lisa with him. All she could do was come outside, then slip away as soon as possible. She took a deep breath and walked down the hall to her doom.

Tex was waiting by the front door. "What were you doing hiding away in there?" he asked. "You should be outside with your guests. And why did you take off that shirt I told you to wear?"

"I . . . uh." Tamera's mind went blank.

Luckily she was saved from coming up with an answer as a group of people came into the house. "Here she is," Tex said heartily. "This is little Tia I wanted you to meet. Say hi to the Robertsons, Tia. This here is Bo, Mary Ellen, and Bayliss."

Tamera smiled and mumbled a hello.

Tex tapped her on the shoulder. "Tia honey, your mother sent me inside to get more chips. Run into the kitchen and bring me out another bag from the counter, please."

"Okay," Tamera said. She crossed the living room and opened what she hoped was the kitchen door. She found herself staring into the broom closet.

"Whoops," she said, turning around to see Tex

and his guests all watching her. "The kitchen—of course. I can never get the hang of this place."

She could see Tex looking at her strangely. "Are you okay, Tia?"

"I'm fine," Tamera said. "You go on out. I'll bring the chips."

She looked around desperately and finally noticed the swing door at the far end of the room. That had to lead to the kitchen. Please let it be the kitchen door, she prayed. It was. She grabbed the bag of chips, wondering if she should take her chance and go hide again, or take them out to Tex. She wondered where Tia was.

Tia had been trying to escape from a group of boring old people who were asking her about gangs in the city. "Excuse me, but I think my mother needs my help," she said at last. She was fleeing across the patio when Tex stopped her.

"Where are the chips?" he asked.

"The chips?"

"I sent you to get them, remember? Have you been drinking, Tia?"

"Of course not," Tia said. "Why are you looking at me like that?"

"You changed your shirt again," Tex said. "Now, please go get the chips."

Tia shrugged and headed for the house. At that moment Lisa grabbed her. "Come with me, honey. Mr. Gonzales wants to meet you."

"Okay, but—" Tia began as Lisa dragged her

through the crowd. "He's really important around here. Be nice to him."

"Mr. Gonzales," Lisa said dramatically, "this is my daughter, Tia."

On the other side of Mr. Gonzales, Tex suddenly appeared. "Mr. Gonzales—you wanted to meet Tia. Here she is!" He had Tamera by the arm.

Mr. Gonzales looked from Tia's face to Tamera's. "Is this some sort of joke?" he asked. "I'm seeing double!"

Tex and Lisa were also staring, open-mouthed.

"Tamera? What are you doing here?" Lisa demanded.

Tia and Tamera gave hopeful smiles. "Surprise," they said together.

When the guests had gone, Tex and Lisa finally sat down with the girls in the living room. Tia and Tamera shot each other nervous glances.

"Mom, Tex, we're really sorry," Tia said. "But we missed each other so much . . ."

"And I was so sure you'd say yes that I went ahead and bought the ticket," Tamera blurted out.

"She had to come," Tia said in a flash of inspiration. "She had nowhere else to go. Ray had made plans with his new girlfriend."

"New girlfriend? What new girlfriend?" Lisa demanded.

"The one he met while you were busy with Tex," Tia said, glancing at Tamera to see how she was doing. "She's really nice, isn't she, Tamera?"

"Very gorgeous," Tamera said, "but nice, too."

"So where has Ray gone with this . . . person?" Lisa demanded.

Tia said, "California," at the same time that Tamera said, "New York."

"He changed his mind at the last minute," Tamera corrected. "They went to New York. She's from there. She's in fashion."

"Your father should have known better than to put you on a plane without talking to me first," Lisa snapped. "That was very irresponsible. I'm going to tell him what I think of him."

Tex touched her knee. "It's okay, honey. The girls obviously missed each other. I can understand that. Don't worry, Tamera. You can stay. It will be nice for Tia to have company."

"Great. Now we can go to work," Tamera said the next morning. "Although I feel kind of weird trying to get Lisa away from Tex when he was so understanding last night."

"You haven't seen his bad side yet," Tia said. "Do you have a plan?"

Tamera went to her bag. "You'll be pleased to know that I did serious research while you were away. I actually went to the library."

"The library? You?"

"Pretty amazing, huh?" Tamera looked pleased. "I never thought I'd ever go into a library when I didn't have to. See how far I'm prepared to go for you?"

"And what did you actually do in the library? Did you manage to find the books?"

"Ha, ha, very funny. You'll be very impressed. I found out all the bad things about North Texas. Rattlesnakes, for example."

"And just how is that going to help us? Where do you think we're going to find a rattlesnake in the whole of North Texas? And we're not exactly going to pick it up and bring it home with us, are we?"

"Of course not," Tamera said, still looking very pleased. "That's why I brought my own."

"You what?"

Tamera reached into the bag. "Ta-da!" Tia jumped backward as Tamera produced a long wriggling rattlesnake.

"Are you crazy?" Tia shrieked.

"Relax, sis. It's only rubber. I got it at a joke shop. Pretty cool, huh?"

"Amazing. It looks so real."

"Yeah, doesn't it? I figure we'll put it under Lisa's chair and she'll be packing her bags in five minutes."

"All right!" Tia said. "For the dumb sister, you're pretty smart sometimes. Let's do it. Lisa takes her coffee out onto the patio when it's sunny."

Trying not to giggle too loudly, the twins crept through the house with the fake rattlesnake in Tia's sports bag. Lisa was sitting on the patio, just as Tia had thought, reading a magazine and drinking coffee.

"This is the life, girls, huh?" she asked, looking up with a big smile. "No rush, no work, someone else scrubbing the floors. Not having to face all that traffic in the city. I could take to this in a hurry."

"Of course, Texas does have its dangerous side, too," Tamera said, sitting down beside Lisa while Tia went around behind her with the rattlesnake and placed it half hidden in the shrubbery.

"Like what?" Lisa demanded.

"Tornadoes, for example. Lots of tornadoes in Texas."

Lisa laughed. "It would take more than a tornado to blow over this house. It's as solid as a rock."

"And poisonous critters," Tamera went on. "Do you know how many rattlesnakes there are around here? They call it the rattlesnake capital of the world."

"You've been watching too much Discovery Channel," Lisa said with a smile. "I haven't even seen a rattlesnake since I got here."

Tamera turned around and gave a little cry. "Ohmygosh, Lisa. I don't believe it, but there's a snake coming out of the bushes right now!"

"Where?" Lisa got to her feet. "I don't see no—Ohmygosh, it is a rattlesnake, and it's huge. Don't anybody move. Don't panic, don't panic!"

As her voice rose, Tex came running out of the house.

"Snake!" Lisa gasped. "There's a big rattlesnake right behind me, Tex. What do I do?"

"Don't move, honey," Tex said. "This'll take care of it."

He vanished into the house, came back with a

shotgun, and fired one shot. "That's how we deal with critters around here," he said. "Now I'll just bury the body and—"

"Wait, Tex." Tia leaped toward the snake. "We've never seen a snake close up. Can't we have a look at it first?"

"Oh no, you don't, little lady," Tex said. "Snakes are dangerous even when dead. Their muscles can still shoot out venom. I can tell you of people who died after getting bit by a dead snake. I'll just pick it up carefully, like this, and . . ."

He stopped and looked at them in disgust. "Why, you've been fooled, Lisa. This snake isn't real. These little brats have been playing a trick on you!"

Tia and Tamera tried to smile.

"Just a joke," Tia said.

"Hope you weren't really scared," Tamera added.

"That's a poor sort of joke," Tex said. "What kind of daughter would want to scare her mother? I don't like that kind of thing, Tia. Don't let it happen again."

"No, sir," Tia said.

"So much for your good idea," Tia said gloomily when they were back in their room. "Now Lisa thinks there are no real snakes and Tex is a hero for saving her."

"I've got more suggestions from my research," Tamera said. "One of them has to work."

"Like what?"

"Like this—it's a cream that attracts mosquitoes.

Lisa won't be so happy here if she gets covered in bites. And I read about fire ants, too. They're all over this area, and if you sit on a fire ants' nest, you know you've been bitten. I saw pictures of fire ants and their nests. I think I could recognize one pretty easily. Now all we have to do is take your mother out for a picnic."

"And we can make her wear those cowboy boots she bought!" Tia exclaimed. "You know, the ones with the very pointed toes? Then we'll go for a hike. She's going to be one crabby person by the time we get home!"

"Detroit will seem like heaven." Tamera laughed.

Tia grabbed her sister's shoulders. "This has to work, Tamera."

Chapter 12

"We should take Tamera out and show her around," Tia suggested to her mother later that morning. "We could go in one of the trucks or on the horses, and have a picnic maybe."

"Tex has some ranch work to do," Lisa said.

"He doesn't have to come. We wouldn't go far," Tia said. "I know my way to the creek. That's a neat place for a picnic."

"Okay, why not?" Lisa said. "I'll see Maria about some food."

"Oh, and Mom—why don't you wear your new outfit for Tamera? She's never seen you in full Western gear."

"You want Tamera to laugh at me, don't you?" Lisa asked, the smile fading from her face.

"No, I don't."

"*You* laughed at me."

"Mom, I don't want Tamera to laugh. I just want her to see you in full Western gear. Nobody will laugh, I promise, and Tex loves to see you dressed that way."

"Well, I suppose I did buy it to wear, didn't I?" Lisa said. "I'll go change."

Half an hour later, they carried the picnic basket to the truck. Tamera opened her bag. "Here, Tia, Lisa, don't forget to put on sunscreen," she said, handing the tube of cream to Lisa. "The sun is very strong out here."

She sneaked a quick glance at Tia as Lisa smeared the cream over her face and arms. Tia took it and pretended to put it on.

They started down the track and then left Tex's property, heading along the road for the creek where Paco had taken Tia.

"Let's park here and walk the rest of the way," Tia said. "It's a lovely little stroll down to the creek."

"Can't we drive all the way down?" Lisa asked.

"It's such a nice day, let's walk," Tamera begged. "Tia and I will carry the blanket."

They got out of the truck. The sun was warm on their backs as they set off down the sandy track. The sand was soft in places and it was hard going.

"How far did you say it was?" Lisa asked, pausing to wipe the sweat from her face.

"Not far," Tia said. "It only took a couple of seconds in the truck."

"I don't even see the creek yet," Lisa said. "My

feet are killing me, and all these bugs keep flying in my face."

Tia gave Tamera a delighted grin.

By the time they reached the creek, they were all sweating.

"I feel like I've been bitten to pieces," Lisa said. "I need to sit down and rest."

"Over here, Lisa," Tamera called. "This is a nice shady place." She caught Tia's eye and mouthed "Fire ants' nest" to her.

Lisa flopped onto the sandy ground. She had been there only a couple of seconds when a strange look came over her face. Suddenly she jumped up, yelling, "Something's biting me. Help—I'm being bitten all over."

Tia and Tamera rushed to her. "Oh no, looks like you sat on a fire ants' nest, Lisa," Tamera said. "Hold still, we'll get them off you."

Lisa was yelling and dancing around as the girls brushed off the little red ants.

"Remind me not to go on any more picnics," Lisa said grouchily after they had removed the last ant. "I'll stick to the ranch house and air conditioning in future."

She went down to the edge of the creek and sat in the shade on Paco's big rock. "This is safer, I think," she said. "No bugs on rocks."

The girls were in the middle of unloading the picnic supplies when Tia froze. "Mom," she said in a low voice, "don't move. There's a snake right by your left foot."

Lisa rolled her eyes as she looked down at the snake. "Oh please, not that one again. You must think I'm very dumb, Tia, if I can't tell the difference between a rubber snake and a real one by now."

"But, Mom—" Tia began as Lisa picked up a stick.

"We'll just flick the mean old snake into the water, shall we, baby?" Lisa teased. She swept the stick under the snake's body and sent it flying through the air to land with a splash in the middle of the creek.

"See?" She laughed. "Wasn't I brave? I'm really great with rubber snakes—" She broke off in horror. The snake was swimming away down the stream, sending wide ripples across the smooth water. "It was real." Lisa gasped. "I touched a real rattlesnake." Her face lit up. "Tex is going to be so proud of me! Now I really am a real Western gal. I can handle rattlesnakes—that wasn't even hard! See, Tia, I knew I belonged out here."

"Let's face it, Tamera. Nothing is going to work." Tia sighed as she lay on her bed later that day. Outside she could hear Lisa going through the snake story one more time in an excited voice. "Every time we try to make her hate it here, she just likes it more."

Tamera nodded. "And she just likes Tex more. I think you have to face the fact that you're stuck here, Tia. The best we can hope for is that I can come and stay for part of the year and you can come to me for part of it."

"If only they'd let me spend the school year with

you," Tia said. "I can't go to school here, Tamera. I'd never get into a good college."

"Then tell your mom that," Tamera said. "She wants the best for you."

"I don't think she's thinking straight right now," Tia said gloomily. "Anything Tex wants, she goes along with."

Tamera lay back with a sigh. "It does look pretty hopeless. I've used up all my great ideas."

Tia got up and went over to Tamera's bed. "Maybe we're going about this the wrong way," she said in a low voice. "Maybe we should be working on Tex."

"To make him stop liking it here and move to Detroit? I don't think so," Tamera said.

"No, stupid—to make him think that marrying my mom isn't such a good idea."

"Yeah, but how do we do that? He thinks she's wonderful. And we don't even know what he likes and doesn't like."

"I could ask Paco," Tia said excitedly. "He knows everything about everybody."

"You're just trying to find an excuse to meet Paco again," Tamera teased.

Tia smiled. "I wouldn't mind. Isn't he nice, Tamera?"

Tamera nodded. "He seemed like a sweet guy."

"And smart, too. And easy to talk to. I don't think I've ever had a guy friend before that I could really talk to as a person and not worry that he was a boy and I was a girl."

"So call him up. Don't worry about me. You don't have to take me with you."

Tia winced. "Slight problem. Tex has forbidden me to see him. So it might be hard to explain where I was if I left you behind."

"Tex really is a jerk," Tamera said. "Your mom has never forbidden you to see a guy, has she? She trusts you. Go ahead and call Paco and find out how we get out of this place."

An hour later the girls hiked to the road and managed to squeeze into Paco's truck.

"I'm so glad you called," Paco said. "I thought maybe that Tex wouldn't let you see me again."

"Tex can say what he likes," Tia said, tossing her head angrily. "I know you're a nice person, and that's good enough for me."

"All the same, I wouldn't want you to get in trouble over me." Paco glanced at her shyly.

Tia smiled at him. "You're worth it," she said.

Tamera looked out of the window and rolled her eyes.

Paco swung the truck onto the track leading to the creek.

"This is where we took Lisa this morning and tried to make her hate Texas," Tamera said. "But it didn't work."

"Nothing is working so far," Tia said. "That's why we need your help, Paco."

"I don't see how I can help," Paco said.

"We thought that our only hope might be to make

Tex decide that marrying Lisa wasn't such a good idea after all," Tamera suggested, leaning across Tia. "Any suggestions?"

The truck stopped and they climbed down onto the warm sand.

"You want me to dress up as Lisa's long-lost husband?" Paco suggested with a grin. "Actually, I've no idea. You don't want to trash your mother, do you?"

"No, I don't."

Paco walked to the edge of the water and stared out thoughtfully. After a while he said, "I don't know why I'm telling you this, because I don't really want you to go, but Tex has a real bad temper. When he loses his cool, he really loses it. He's famous around here."

"Paco, that's great!" Tamera exclaimed. "Now all we have to do is make Tex lose his cool." She turned to Tia. "We should be able to do that, right? We've driven everyone else in the world crazy, haven't we?"

"We can show Tex what it's like living with two teenagers in the house." Tia danced around excitedly. "I'll tell him that you have to come to stay with us, at least part of the year. Then we'll act like brats, and he'll decide that he won't marry my mom if it means being stuck with me."

"You'll be out of here before you know it!" Tamera yelled.

Tia's smile faded as she saw Paco's face. She reached out and touched his arm. "I'm sorry, Paco," she said. "If it makes you feel any better, you are the only reason I'd want to stay here."

Paco managed a smile. "It's okay," he said. "I don't want you to go, but I know it's better for you if you do. I hope your little scheme works."

"You're looking at Tia and Tamera, the dynamic duo," Tamera said, chuckling. "When we work together, we're unstoppable. Tex won't know what's hit him!"

Chapter 13

The next morning the twins put their plan into action. Tia waited until she heard her mother in the shower, then she went up to Tex at the breakfast table.

"I want to thank you for letting me have Tamera here," she said. "Now I feel I can relax and be my-self again."

"I'm glad to hear that," Tex said. "I got the feeling that you didn't like it here."

"That was only because it was all so new and I was feeling shy," Tia said. "Now that Tamera's here, everything is great." She perched on the table beside him and leaned across to butter herself a piece of toast. "You have no idea how lost I feel without my sister," Tia went on. "In fact, I don't think I could survive without her. If we come to live here, I hope you'll let me have Tamera stay during the vacations."

"Sure you can," Tex said. "No problem."

"Thanks, Tex. I'll go tell Tamera," Tia said. She got up, leaving the toast, with a bite out of it, on the tablecloth. She walked as far as the hallway. "Hey, Tamera, guess what?" she yelled at the top of her voice. "Tex says you can stay here whenever you like!"

"Chillin'!" Tamera yelled back. She came out of Tia's room. "Of course, now that you're going to be living here, you can start making this place more like home. It's so boring right now. You need to put up posters on all the walls and bring all your rap CDs."

"Yeah," Tia said. "I really miss my music. This place is too quiet."

"I brought a couple of CDs with me," Tamera said. "You want me to go put one on?"

She ran back into Tia's bedroom. Soon a great blast of sound came from the CD player. The whole house throbbed to a heavy rap beat.

"Hey, that's too loud, Tia," Tex said, looking up from his breakfast. "Tell your sister to turn it down."

"Loud? This?" Tia shouted. "This is how we always listen to music at home. We play it all the time like this, night and day."

Tamera came back with arms full of clothes. "Look at this stuff, Tia," she said. "None of it is suitable for living here. We'll have to go shopping for new clothes. Ask your mom if she can drive us into Dallas today. You need a complete new wardrobe."

"I don't know," Tia said. "This is okay, isn't it?" She held up a denim jacket. Then she shook her head. "Nah. Too old." She dropped it on the floor.

"What about this?" Tamera asked, holding up a tie-dyed T-shirt. "Too seventies, right?" She threw it onto the sofa.

"I guess you're right," Tia said. "It *is* all wrong. Let's go get my mom out of the shower and tell her I need all new stuff." She dropped the rest of the clothing. They headed in the direction of Lisa's room, leaving clothes all over the furniture and floor.

"Hey, wait a second," Tex yelled after them. "What about all this stuff?"

"Oh, that?" Tia said, eyeing it with a look of disgust. "It's old. I don't want it anymore."

"You can't just leave it here," Tex growled.

"You want me to pick it up? Now?" Tia whined. "Later, okay?"

Then she and Tamera walked on down the hallway to Lisa's room.

"Did you see his face?" Tamera whispered. "We were really bugging him. I think this is working just great."

By the end of the day, Tex's nerves were definitely beginning to look frazzled.

"Let's watch a video tonight, okay?" Tamera suggested.

"Okay," Tia said, and noticed that Tex and Lisa looked relieved.

"But we need popcorn first," Tia said. "I'll go make some."

"Do you need help?" Lisa asked nervously.

"It's okay. We can do it," Tamera said. "I'll help Tia."

They went into the kitchen and took down every bowl they could find. When they had popped the corn in the microwave, they drizzled melted butter over it and over most of the counter. Then they came out again, grabbing handfuls of corn as they walked. Half the corn missed their mouths and dropped onto the floor.

"Hey, watch it, girls," Lisa called after them. "You're making a mess."

"That's okay. Maria can sweep it up in the morning," Tia said breezily.

"Maria doesn't come here to clean up after you, young lady," Tex said coldly.

"I thought she was the maid. Isn't that what maids do—clean up after the family?" Tia said. She sounded so convincing that even Tamera swallowed hard.

"Come on, Tamera. Let's go find a rock video," Tia went on.

When they were inside Tia's room, they both started giggling nervously, staring at each other in horror at the way they were acting.

"How are we doing, do you think?" Tia asked.

"He looked like he was about to explode," Tamera said delightedly.

"I feel bad, acting like this," Tia said, "but I don't know what else to do."

"You have to go through with it," Tamera agreed. "Now that his nerves are frazzled, we just have to come up with something bad enough to make him really blow his top."

"I've never done anything really bad in my whole life," Tia said. "Any suggestions?"

"Smuggle Paco into your room?"

Tia shook her head. "No, I'm not getting Paco in trouble. And I don't want to come across like a real rebel, just a normal teenager. I want Tex to think this is what it's going to be like every day from now on. What do normal kids do that bugs adults?"

"They fight," Tamera said.

"We hardly ever fight," Tia said.

"I bet we would have fought all the time if we'd been together as little kids."

"Better late than never," Tia said with a knowing grin. She picked up Tamera's beret, which was lying on the dresser. "You brought this hat with you?" she yelled loudly. "Boy, do you have a nerve! You know it's mine."

"It is not!"

"Is, too!"

"Nuh-uh. Yours is navy blue. This one is black."

"That's navy blue! Are you color blind?"

"It's black and it's mine and you're not having it!" Tamera yelled.

Tia ran out into the living room. "Mom, Tamera's got my favorite hat, and she won't give it to me, and she says it's hers."

Tamera appeared behind her, clutching the hat. "It is mine. Hers is navy blue."

"That one's mine. I know it!" Tia yelled. "Hers is different. Make her give it to me now."

"Tia, calm down and stop acting like a baby," Lisa said. "What's gotten into you?"

"I'm just fed up with Tamera taking my things without asking me."

"Huh, who took my lacy blouse that time, Miss Perfect?" Tamera countered.

"That was different. I would have asked you, but you were hanging with your friends at the dumb mall."

"At least I wasn't doing boring experiments in the science lab at school with a bunch of geeks."

"Don't you call my friends geeks!"

"That's what they are!" Tamera shouted.

Tex got up. "Stop this right now! I won't have this fighting in my living room."

"It's okay," Tamera said. "We do it all the time at home. We can't help it. Twins are like that."

"Just make her give me the hat and I'll stop," Tia said. She wriggled past Tex and made a grab at Tamera. "Give it to me!"

"Have to catch me first!" Tamera yelled, and dodged away.

They rushed around the furniture, screaming while Tex and Lisa tried to stop them. Finally Tia had Tamera backed into a corner. "Give me that!" she yelled.

"Okay, go get it," Tamera said, laughing. She threw the hat over Tia's head. It landed on one of the Native American pots. The pot fell to the floor and smashed into little pieces. Tia and Tamera stood there, too horrified to move.

Tex leaped across the room. "You little brats, look what you've done!" he yelled. "You're monsters, both of you! You just wait until I'm your father, Tia. I'll soon teach you how to behave properly. It will be boarding school for you—the strictest one I can find! And don't think I'm going to let your spoiled brat of a sister come here again. She's out of here tomorrow, do you hear me?"

His voice had risen until it echoed through the room. He towered over Tia, shaking his fist at her. Tia was so frightened that she could hardly breathe. She knew their plan had been to push Tex until he lost his temper, but she had never stopped to think how scary he might be. What if he did send her to a strict boarding school? What if he never allowed her to see Tamera again?

Then Lisa stepped between Tex and Tia. "Don't you dare yell at my baby like that," she said in a threatening voice. She stood there with her hands on her hips, her eyes blazing. "Nobody is allowed to yell at my baby, except me—understand?"

"Your baby is a brat!" Tex yelled at Lisa. "You have spoiled her and babied her and look at the result—she's totally out of control." His voice softened. "Of course, I don't entirely blame you. If only you'd had a man around to guide you, you'd have known how to keep her in line."

"Excuse me?" Lisa said coldly.

"Honey, everyone knows that it takes a man to be

head of the family and make the rules," Tex said, talking to her as if she were a little child. "Women are too soft with the kids. But don't worry—I'm here to guide you now. I'll soon get this kid shaped up, now that I'm the boss."

Lisa was still standing like a statue, staring at him. "Don't you worry," she said, "because Tia won't be around to be shaped up. She'll be back home with me in Detroit, where we belong." She looked at Tia. "Go pack your things, honey. We're going home in the morning."

The next morning they stood outside the ranch house as Jose carried their bags to the Explorer. Tia knew that she should be feeling happy, but instead there was a big lump inside her throat that wouldn't go away. Tex hadn't said a word to any of them since the night before. At the last minute Tia ran inside to find him. He was in his office, staring at a computer screen.

"I'm sorry about last night," Tia blurted. "I feel really bad that we broke your pot. We didn't mean to. I'll send you the money from my allowance to replace it."

Tex looked up from the computer screen. "You never wanted your mama to marry me, did you?"

Tia looked down, embarrassed.

"Well, you got what you wanted, didn't you? I hope you're feeling real good about it."

"I'm sorry," Tia said, "but I didn't just do it for me. It was obvious that she didn't belong out here.

She's a city girl, she's loud and feisty and she does her own thing. She was trying to turn into a person she wasn't."

Tex sighed. "Maybe you're right. I just thought . . ."

"I have to go," Tia said awkwardly, feeling that she might change her mind at any second and agree that Lisa belonged there after all. "Bye, Tex."

She couldn't get out of there fast enough.

"I'm sorry, Mom," Tia said quietly as they drove down the track to the road. "I guess I really screwed up your life for you. I hope you're not too mad at me."

Lisa looked back at the ranch house, then shook her head. "I guess it went to my head, thinking I could be queen of the ranch. And Tex was a great-looking guy and rich, too. It would have gone to any woman's head."

"But it wasn't right for you, Mom," Tia said. "Tamera and I could see that. That's why we did everything we could to make you see you were making a mistake."

Lisa looked from one twin to the other. "You sure did, didn't you? Snakes and ants and broken vases—you guys are dangerous when you want something. You stop at nothing, don't you?"

"Only because we care about you, Lisa," Tamera said. "You'd have hated it here. Three hours to go shopping? Nothing to do all day except follow Tex around?"

They were almost into Buckeye. Suddenly Tia

leaned forward and touched Jose's shoulder. "Jose, wait a second," she said. "I need to stop here for a moment."

The car screeched to a halt.

"Where are you going, honey?" Lisa asked as Tia jumped down.

"I'll be back in a second," she said. "I have to say goodbye to someone."

Tamera noticed that Paco's truck was parked outside the general store. Tia ran into the store. Paco was waiting out at the feed lot, behind the store. He looked up in surprise when he saw her, and a big smile spread across his face. The smile almost broke Tia's heart.

"Hi, what are you doing here?" he asked. "Come to buy some cattle feed?"

"Paco, I've come to say goodbye," Tia said softly. "We're on our way to the airport."

"You're leaving, for good?"

Tia nodded. "You were right. Your idea worked. Tex lost his temper, and my mother decided that she couldn't live with him after all."

"So you're going back where you belong?" Paco said softly.

"I'll miss you," Tia said.

"I won't ever forget you," he said.

"And I won't ever forget you. I just wish we'd had time to get to know each other better. I think we could have become good friends."

"You already are my good friend," Paco said simply.

"I'll write to you," Tia said. "Maybe you could come visit in the summer."

"Maybe," Paco said. Tia realized right away that he wouldn't have the money for the fare.

"And promise me one thing," Tia said.

"What?"

"You won't ever give up your dreams. You'll go to college and you'll keep on writing. Who knows, one day you'll be a famous author and you'll come to talk at the Detroit library and I'll meet you again and ask for your autograph." She could feel tears running down her cheeks.

Paco nodded, trying to smile. "Maybe we'll go to the same college—we'll both be at Rice together."

"Rice? We'll both be at Harvard," Tia said with a laugh. She looked around. "I have to go, Paco. They're all waiting outside."

"Thanks for coming to say goodbye, Tia."

"Bye, Paco," Tia said. She leaned forward and brushed his lips in a gentle kiss. Then, before he could say or do anything more, she broke away from him and ran out to the waiting car.

"Guess what, Tia?" Tamera said excitedly as she climbed back in and they drove off. "We might still have time to go to Disney World for a couple of days."

"I thought your father was in New York with his new girlfriend," Lisa said.

"I have a feeling he might have decided to come home early, just like us," Tamera said. "Wouldn't that be great, huh, Tia? You and me on Space Mountain?"

"What?" Tia asked. She looked blankly at Tamera.

"I guess it was hard saying goodbye, wasn't it?" Tamera asked gently.

Tia swallowed hard and nodded. She brushed back her tears as they drove across the flat dry landscape toward the skyscrapers of Dallas glittering on the horizon.

"I don't know what got into me," Lisa said, bright and bouncy again as she saw Dallas ahead of them. "What made me think that I'd be happy out in the boonies? I'd have died of boredom in a month. And if that man had tried to boss me around . . ." She broke off and looked at Tia. "You did your best to warn me, didn't you, honey? Well, you were right. You and I belong in the city, and that's where we're going to stay." A spasm of alarm came over her face. "If we still can, of course."

"What do you mean?" Tia asked.

Lisa turned to look at Tia and Tamera in the backseat. "I mean if Ray hasn't decided to marry the fashion princess he went to New York with this week."

"But he didn't really—" Tamera began.

Tia kicked her and said, more loudly, "I don't think so. She's not his type. Too quiet and boring. He likes feisty women."

"That's okay then," Lisa said with a little smile. "One feisty woman coming home."

Tamera nudged Tia. "Three feisty women coming home," she said.

About the Author

Janet Quin-Harkin has written over fifty books for teenagers, including the best-seller *Ten-Boy Summer*. She is the author of several popular series: TGIF!, Friends, Heartbreak Café, Senior Year, and The Boyfriend Club. She has also written several romances.

Ms. Quin-Harkin lives with her husband in San Rafael, California. She has four children. In addition to writing books, she teaches creative writing at a nearby college.